CHRONICLE CHIMES

A MYSTICAL JOURNEY THROUGH CAPTIVATING STORIES AND ADVENTURES.

SUBHASMITA PANDA

To the dreamers and seekers of truth, whose hearts resonate with the whispers of history. May this book be a testament to your courage to explore the past and embrace the future.To my family, whose love and support have been my foundation; your unwavering faith in my journey fuels my passion. To my friends, who have been my companions through every twist and turn, thank you for your encouragement and laughter.

To every reader who opens these pages, may you find inspiration in the stories shared and courage to follow your own path. Let the chimes of time remind us that every moment is a chance to create, learn, and grow.

Contents

Contents

Contents

Contents

Contents

What Is Life ?

Life is a canvas, painted with dreams,
A tapestry woven with laughter and screams.
Through trials we wander, through joy we ignite,
In the journey of living, we find our true light.

Acknowledgements

As I reflect on the journey of writing "**Chronicle Chimes,**" I am filled with gratitude for the many individuals who have supported me along the way. This book is a culmination of shared experiences, insights, and encouragement, and it would not have been possible without the contributions of so many. First and foremost, I extend my deepest appreciation to my family. To my parents, thank you for instilling in me a love for storytelling and for always believing in my dreams. Your unwavering support has been my guiding light, and your sacrifices have made this journey possible. To my siblings, your laughter and encouragement have kept me grounded and inspired me to reach for the stars.

To my friends, both near and far, I am grateful for your patience during the countless hours spent writing and revising. Your willingness to listen to my ideas, provide feedback, and share in my excitement has made this process not only enjoyable but profoundly rewarding. Thank you for reminding me to celebrate the small victories along the way. I owe a special debt of gratitude to my mentors and fellow writers. Your guidance and wisdom have shaped my understanding of the craft and pushed me to improve my skills. Each conversation and critique has been invaluable, offering new perspectives that I carry with me in every word I write.

To my editor, I cannot thank you enough for your expertise and insight. Your meticulous attention to detail and constructive feedback have transformed my initial drafts into a cohesive narrative. Your belief in this project has inspired me to elevate my writing to new heights.

ACKNOWLEDGEMENTS

Lastly, to the readers—thank you for choosing to embark on this journey with me. Your willingness to engage with these stories means the world to me. I hope that **"Chronicle Chimes"** resonates with you and inspires reflection, connection, and a sense of wonder about the world around us.Each of you has played a crucial role in this endeavor, and I am eternally grateful for your support. This book is as much yours as it is mine.

Foreword

In a world that often rushes forward, it is essential to pause and listen—to the stories that shape us, the histories that inform our present, and the echoes of the past that guide our future. "**Chronicle Chimes**" invites you to embark on a journey through time, exploring the rich tapestry of experiences that connect us all. This book is a celebration of moments, memories, and the profound lessons they impart. Each chapter resonates with the rhythm of life's experiences, encouraging readers to reflect on their own journeys while engaging with the narratives woven within these pages. The author's insightful prose invites us to delve deeper, revealing the beauty found in both joy and sorrow.

As you turn the pages, you will encounter a diverse array of voices and perspectives, each contributing to a greater understanding of our shared humanity. This work serves as a reminder that while our stories may differ, the threads that bind us are universal.

I encourage you to immerse yourself in the stories of "**Chronicle Chimes.**" Let the words resonate with you, inspire contemplation, and perhaps even spark a new chapter in your own life. This book is more than a collection of tales; it is an invitation to reflect, connect, and grow. May you find within these pages the echoes of your own experiences and the inspiration to continue your journey forward.

Preface

Welcome to **"Chronicle Chimes,"** a collection of reflections, stories, and insights that seeks to capture the essence of our shared human experience. As I embarked on this journey of writing, I found myself drawn to the moments that define us—those fleeting instances that resonate deeply, echoing through time.

This book is a culmination of my thoughts and observations, inspired by the rich tapestry of life that surrounds us. Each chapter delves into themes of connection, memory, and the lessons learned from both joy and hardship. Through these narratives, I hope to illuminate the intricate ways in which our past informs our present and shapes our future.

Writing **"Chronicle Chimes"** has been both a personal and transformative experience. It has allowed me to reflect on my own journey while also honoring the stories of others that have influenced my path. I believe that storytelling has the power to foster understanding and empathy, bridging the gaps between our diverse experiences.As you read, I encourage you to engage with the stories and consider the echoes of your own life. Each of us carries a unique narrative, and in sharing these moments, we connect with one another in profound ways.

Thank you for joining me on this exploration. May **"Chronicle Chimes"** resonate with you and inspire you to reflect on the stories that shape your own journey.

Prologue

In the quiet moments between past and present, where memories linger like shadows, we find the echoes of our lives. "Chronicle Chimes" invites you into this space—a realm where stories intertwine and the essence of time is captured in fleeting moments.

Every chapter within this book is a reflection of the human experience, exploring themes of love, loss, resilience, and discovery. These narratives are not merely tales; they are the chimes of our collective history, resonating with the rhythm of our shared existence.

As you turn the pages, you will encounter characters who face challenges that mirror our own, who seek understanding in a world that often feels chaotic and unpredictable. Their journeys are a reminder that while we may walk different paths, the emotions we experience are universal.

This prologue serves as a doorway into the heart of the book, inviting you to pause, reflect, and listen to the stories that unfold. Let the chimes of these chronicles remind you of the power of connection and the beauty found in the intricacies of life. May you find within these pages a sense of belonging and inspiration, a call to embrace your own story as part of the greater narrative of humanity.

EMBRACING LIFE'S JOURNEY: A STORY OF RESILIENCE AND GROWTH

FAILURE CAN LEAD TO SUCCESS

From the serene days of my childhood, I recall the laughter that echoed through our home, the warmth of family bonds, and the innocence that painted my world in hues of wonder. Growing up in a nurturing environment, I learned the values of kindness, resilience, and perseverance, laying the foundation for the journey ahead. Born in a small town nestled between rolling hills, I came into the world with a curiosity that seemed to know no bounds. From an early age, I was drawn to exploration, whether it was the hidden corners of our backyard or the mysteries of the books that lined our shelves. My parents, nurturing and supportive, encouraged this inquisitive spirit, laying the foundation for a life driven by a thirst for knowledge and understanding.

As I grew, so too did my appetite for discovery. School became my playground, each lesson an opportunity to uncover something new about the world and myself. I thrived on the challenge of learning, eagerly immersing myself in subjects ranging from literature to mathematics, soaking up every bit of information like a sponge. Education became my beacon of hope, a gateway to a brighter future. With determination as my compass, I navigated through the corridors of learning, fueled by a thirst for knowledge and a desire to carve my path in this vast world.Excelled academically, driven by a passion for discovery.

Explored various interests, from arts to sciences, fostering creativity.

Developed strong relationships with mentors who guided personal and academic growth.

Life's milestones marked my path, each one a stepping stone toward self-discovery and growth. From the excitement of my first day of school to the bittersweet farewells of secondary education, each experience sculpted the person I am today. But life wasn't all textbooks and equations. Like everyone, I faced my fair share of obstacles along the way. Whether it was navigating the complexities of friendships or grappling with self-doubt, each setback served as a lesson in resilience and determination. Through it all, I learned the importance of perseverance, of pushing forward even when the path seemed daunting. But life has a funny way of throwing curveballs when you least expect it. Just as

I was gaining momentum in my career, tragedy struck, throwing me off course and forcing me to confront my own mortality. In the wake of loss, I found solace in the simple things: the warmth of the sun on my face, the laughter of loved ones, the gentle embrace of a friend. It was in these moments of quiet reflection that I discovered the true meaning of resilience—not the ability to bounce back, but the courage to move forward, even in the face of uncertainty.

Emotional moments cast shadows on my journey, testing my resolve and resilience. From moments of doubt to heartaches that felt insurmountable, I learned to embrace vulnerability as a catalyst for growth, understanding that even in darkness, there exists the promise of dawn.

Motivational moments breathed life into my aspirations, igniting the flames of ambition within me. Whether it was the encouraging words of a mentor or the silent whispers of my own dreams, I drew strength from the belief that anything is possible with unwavering determination.

Hard work became my mantra, the cornerstone of my journey towards success. With every obstacle I faced, I embraced the challenge, knowing that perseverance and dedication are the keys to unlocking the doors of opportunity. Support, both from loved ones and mentors, became my lifeline, offering guidance, encouragement, and solace in moments of uncertainty. Their belief in my abilities fueled my determination, reminding me that I am never alone in this pursuit of greatness.

Through it all, a singular goal illuminated my path: to make a difference, to leave an indelible mark on the world. With unwavering focus and unyielding determination, I pursued my dreams, knowing that the journey itself is as meaningful as the destination. And finally, success became not merely a destination but a testament to the resilience of the human spirit. With humility as my compass, I celebrate not only my achievements but also the lessons learned, the obstacles overcome, and the relationships forged along the way. In the tapestry of life, each thread represents a moment, a choice, a journey. And as I reflect upon my own story, I am reminded that it is not the destination that defines us, but rather the journey we undertake, the lives we touch, and the legacy we leave behind.

Today, as I look back on the winding road that has brought me to where I am, I am filled with gratitude for the journey and all its twists and turns. Each triumph and tribulation has shaped me into the person I am today: resilient, compassionate, and endlessly curious. As I stand on the threshold of tomorrow, I am filled with excitement for the adventures that lie ahead, knowing that whatever challenges may come my way, I am more than capable of facing them head-on, armed with the lessons of the past and the boundless optimism of the future. This condensed life story captures the essence of a journey filled with ups and downs, highlighting the resilience and growth that comes with navigating through life's challenges and triumphs.

A JOURNEY THROUGH THE WORLD OF PAINTING

In the heart of a bustling city, amidst the chaos of everyday life, there existed a small, unassuming art gallery. Its name whispered amongst the creative circles, was "Canvas Dreams." Though its exterior was modest, within its walls lay a realm of wonder—a world where paintings transcended mere colors and strokes, and each canvas held a story waiting to be told.

The gallery's owner, an enigmatic figure known only as Madame Eloise, possessed a keen eye for talent. She curated the most extraordinary pieces, each one carefully selected to evoke emotions and stir the soul. Among her prized possessions was an ancient painting rumored to hold mystical powers—a portal to other realms.

One rainy afternoon, a young woman named Maya stumbled upon Canvas Dreams. Drawn by an inexplicable force, she stepped inside, her senses overwhelmed by the kaleidoscope of colors and emotions that greeted her. As she wandered through the gallery, each painting seemed to beckon her closer, whispering tales of adventure.

Mesmerized by the artistry before her, Maya found herself standing before the legendary painting—the one rumored to hold the key to other worlds. Without hesitation, she reached out and touched the canvas, her fingertips tingling with anticipation. In a flash of light, the world around her dissolved, and she was whisked away on a journey through the realm of painting.

Her first stop was a lush forest bathed in golden sunlight. Vibrant foliage swayed in the breeze, and exotic creatures roamed freely. With each step, Maya felt a sense of wonder wash over her as if she had been transported to a forgotten paradise. She marveled at the beauty surrounding her, knowing she was experiencing something magical.

As she ventured deeper into the forest, Maya stumbled upon a clearing where a majestic waterfall cascaded into a crystal-clear pool. The sight took her breath away, and she couldn't resist the urge to dive in. The water was cool against her skin, and she laughed with delight as she swam beneath the shimmering surface.Emerging from the pool, Maya stood on the vast desert's shores, where sand dunes stretched as far as the eye could see. The heat was intense, but she pressed on, her curiosity driving her forward. Soon, she stumbled upon a hidden oasis—a sanctuary of lush greenery nestled amidst the barren landscape.

In the heart of the oasis stood a magnificent palace, its towers reaching towards the sky. Maya approached cautiously, unsure of what lay within. To her surprise, the palace was not abandoned but teeming with life. She was welcomed with open arms by the inhabitants, who regaled her with tales of ancient legends and forgotten mysteries.

As Maya continued her journey through the world of painting, she encountered a myriad of landscapes and characters, each more fantastical than the last. She experienced the full spectrum of human emotion from snowy mountain-tops to bustling marketplaces—joy, sorrow, love, and longing.

But as her adventure drew to a close, Maya couldn't shake the feeling that something was missing. Despite the wonders she had witnessed, a part of her longed for the familiar comforts of home. With a heavy heart, she returned to Canvas Dreams, the echoes of her journey still lingering in her mind.

As she stepped back into the gallery, Maya was greeted by Madame Eloise, who smiled knowingly. "You have seen things that most can only dream of," she said, her voice soft but full of wisdom. "But remember, true beauty lies not in the places we visit, but in the journey itself."

With those words ringing in her ears, Maya bid farewell to Canvas Dreams, knowing that she would forever carry the memories of her journey through the world of painting in her heart. As she stepped out into the bustling city once more, she did so with a newfound appreciation for the magic that lay hidden in the most unexpected of places.

IN PURSUIT OF TRUTH : THE DEDICATION OF A JOURNALIST

In the bustling city of Metropolis, amidst the cacophony of honking horns and bustling crowds, stood a figure whose determination and passion outshone the neon lights of the skyscrapers. Her name was Sarah Wells, a seasoned journalist whose unwavering commitment to uncovering the truth had become her life's purpose. Sarah had always been drawn to the written word. As a child, she devoured books, immersing herself in tales of adventure, mystery, and discovery. Her love for storytelling only grew as she matured, leading her to pursue a career in journalism. From the moment she stepped foot into a newsroom, Sarah knew she had found her calling. She thrived in the fast-paced environment, fueled by the adrenaline of chasing leads and uncovering hidden truths. Journalism wasn't just a job for Sarah—it was a passion, a purpose, a way of life.

UNVAILING THE TRUTH

Sarah's journey into journalism began during her college years. While her peers pursued lucrative careers in finance or technology, Sarah found herself drawn to the art of storytelling. She was captivated by the power of words to shed light on the darkest corners of society and to give voice to the voiceless. Her dedication to her craft was unparalleled. While others clocked out at the end of the day, Sarah remained glued to her desk, tirelessly researching, writing, and fact-checking. She sacrificed sleep, socializing, and sometimes even sanity in pursuit of the perfect story. But Sarah's commitment went beyond the confines of her office. She ventured into dangerous territories, risking life and limb to shine a light on the darkest corners of society. From war-torn regions to crime-riddled neighborhoods, Sarah fearlessly pursued stories that others would shy away from.

Her tenacity often put her in harm's way. She narrowly escaped gunfire in conflict zones, dodged threats from powerful figures, and endured countless sleepless nights haunted by the horrors she had witnessed. Yet, despite the risks, Sarah refused to back down. For her, the truth was worth any price.

It wasn't just the thrill of the chase that drove Sarah—it was the impact of her work. She had seen firsthand the power of journalism to effect change, to expose injustices, and to give voice to the voiceless. Each story she broke was a small victory in the fight for a better world.

Fresh out of college, Sarah landed her first job at the Metropolis Gazette, a reputable newspaper known for its fearless investigative reporting. From day one, Sarah threw herself into her work with boundless energy and enthusiasm. She spent long hours poring over documents, chasing leads, and conducting interviews, fueled by her insatiable curiosity and desire for justice.

One of Sarah's most memorable assignments came when she was tasked with investigating corruption within the city government. Despite facing threats and intimidation from powerful figures, Sarah remained undeterred. She followed the trail of breadcrumbs, unearthing evidence of embezzlement and bribery that went all the way to the top.

Her exposé sent shockwaves through the city, leading to widespread reforms and the indictment of several high-ranking officials. But for Sarah, the real victory was knowing that she had made a difference, that her words had sparked change and held the powerful accountable. However, not all of Sarah's stories ended in triumph. There were moments of heartbreak and frustration, times when the truth seemed elusive and justice out of reach. But even in the face of adversity, Sarah refused to give up. She saw herself not just as a reporter, but as a guardian of democracy, fighting to uphold the principles of transparency and accountability.

One such moment came when Sarah uncovered evidence of police brutality in the city's marginalized communities. Despite facing pushback from law enforcement and skepticism from the public, Sarah persisted, shining a spotlight on a systemic issue that had long been ignored. Her reporting sparked a national conversation about race and policing, ultimately leading to reforms aimed at addressing the root causes of inequality.

Through it all, Sarah remained guided by her unwavering dedication to the truth. She understood the power of journalism to shape public discourse and hold the powerful accountable, and she refused to compromise her principles for the sake of convenience or popularity.

As the years went by, Sarah's reputation as a fearless journalist continued to grow. She won numerous awards for her investigative reporting and earned the respect of her peers and colleagues. But for Sarah, the greatest reward was knowing that she had made a difference, that her words had the power to change hearts and minds.

And so, as the sun set on another day in Metropolis, Sarah Wells continued her quest for truth, undeterred by the challenges that lay ahead. For her, journalism was not just a job, but a calling—a sacred duty to shine a light in the darkest of places and to never stop fighting for a better world.

CHAPTER FOUR

THE JOURNEY OF CREATION : FROM PAINT BRUSH TO PEN

In the quaint town of **Riverside**, nestled along the banks of the winding Serenity **River**, lived a young artist named Emily. From a tender **age**, she was entranced by the vibrant colors dancing on her canvas, each stroke telling a story of its own. Yet, beneath her passion for painting lay an unspoken desire to explore the world of words, to weave tales that echoed the melodies of her heart.

Emily's studio was a sanctuary, adorned with splashes of colors and the aroma of freshly squeezed paint. Every morning, she would lose herself in the canvas, capturing the essence of nature's beauty with her trusty paintbrush. But as the sun dipped below the horizon, a different longing whispered in her soul—the urge to put her thoughts into words, to paint with the palette of language.

One evening, as she sat by the window, watching the stars sprinkle the night sky with their twinkling brilliance, inspiration struck her like a bolt of lightning.

With trembling hands, she reached for a blank sheet of paper and a quill, hesitant yet determined to embark on a new journey—into the realm of storytelling.

The words flowed like a river, each sentence weaving a tapestry of emotions and dreams. From the depths of her imagination emerged characters, each with a tale waiting to be told. As the night waned into dawn, Emily's passion for painting found a companion in the art of writing, and the lines between the two blurred into a symphony of creativity.

Her first story, "The Whispering Woods," breathed life into the ancient trees that guarded the secrets of the forest. With each word, she painted a vivid picture of adventure and discovery, inviting readers to lose themselves in the enchanting world she had crafted.

Word of Emily's talent spread like wildfire through the town, drawing curious souls to her doorstep, eager to witness the magic she spun with her pen. Yet, amidst the newfound acclaim, she remained humble, her heart still tethered to the canvas that had been her first love.

As days turned into weeks and weeks into months, Emily's dual passion for painting and writing flourished, each art form fueling the other in an endless cycle of creativity. Her studio became a sanctuary not only for her but for kindred spirits who sought solace in the beauty of expression.

With each stroke of her paintbrush and every stroke of her pen, Emily discovered a piece of herself she never knew existed—a boundless well of imagination waiting to be explored. Through her art, she found a voice that resonated with the hearts of those around her, bridging the gap between dreams and reality.

Years passed, and Emily's legacy grew, her stories and paintings adorning galleries and bookshelves far and wide. Yet, amidst the accolades and acclaim, she remained rooted in the simple joys of creation, finding fulfillment not in fame but in the act of bringing her visions to life.

And so, the chronicles of creativity continued, a never-ending journey of discovery and inspiration. For Emily, the paintbrush and the pen were not mere tools but vessels through which she could explore the vast expanse of her imagination, leaving behind a trail of beauty and wonder for generations to come.

CHAPTER FIVE

THE JOURNEY OF A SCIENCE STUDENT: FROM CURIOSITY TO DISCOVERY

Once upon a time, in a small town nestled between rolling hills and whispering forests, there lived a young girl named Meera. From a tender age, Meera was fascinated by the world around her. She would spend hours exploring the woods, collecting specimens, and marveling at the intricate patterns of nature.

As she grew older, her passion for science blossomed. She devoured books on biology, chemistry, and physics, hungry for knowledge that would unlock the mysteries of the universe. Her teachers noticed her insatiable curiosity and encouraged her to pursue her dreams.

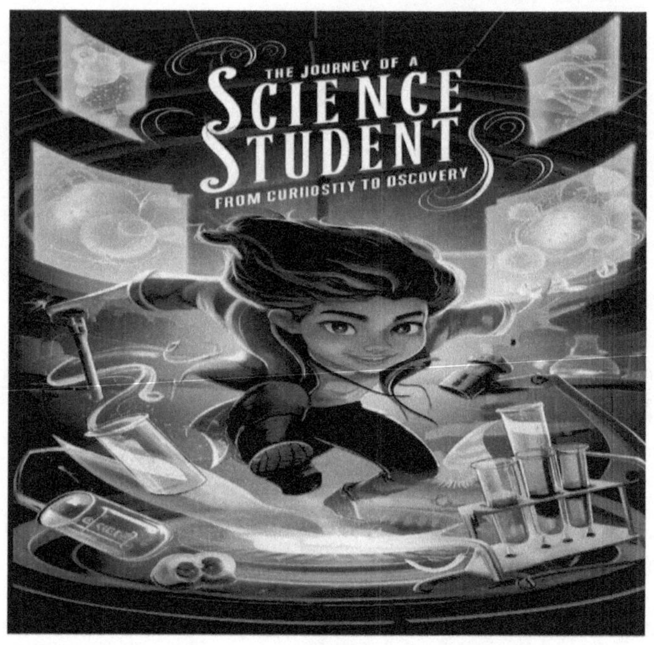

LIFE OF A SCIENCE STUDENT

In high school, Meera's love for science only deepened. She spent countless hours in the laboratory, conducting experiments and uncovering the secrets of the natural world. Whether it was dissecting a frog or mixing chemicals in test tubes, Meera approached each task with boundless enthusiasm and determination.

Despite facing challenges along the way, Meera never wavered in her pursuit of knowledge. She juggled her studies with extracurricular activities, participating in science fairs and competitions, where her innovative projects often earned her recognition and praise.

As graduation approached, Meera faced a difficult decision. With so many paths before her, she wasn't sure which direction to take. Should she study biology and delve deeper into the mysteries of life? Or perhaps chemistry, where she could explore the building blocks of matter? In the end, she followed her heart and enrolled in a prestigious university to pursue a degree in physics.

University life was a whirlwind of lectures, labs, and late-night study sessions. Meera thrived in this environment, surrounded by like-minded individuals who shared her passion for discovery. She formed close bonds with her classmates and professors, who challenged and inspired her to push the boundaries of her knowledge.

Throughout her undergraduate years, Meera immersed herself in research projects, eager to make her mark on the scientific community. From studying the behavior of subatomic particles to unraveling the mysteries of the cosmos, she threw herself into each endeavor with gusto, fueled by a burning desire to unravel the secrets of the universe. As graduation loomed once again,Meera found herself faced with another crossroads. Should she pursue a career in academia, where she could continue her research and inspire the next generation of scientists? Or perhaps she should explore opportunities in industry, where her skills could be put to practical use in solving real-world problems?

After much soul-searching, Meera decided to pursue a Ph.D. in astrophysics, where she could combine her love of physics with her fascination for the cosmos. Over the next few years, she delved deep into her research, studying the origins of stars and galaxies, and the fundamental forces that govern the universe. But as she delved deeper into her studies, Meera began to feel a sense of disillusionment. The more she learned, the more questions arose, and the more daunting the task ahead seemed. Was she truly making a difference? Would her research ever lead to meaningful discoveries, or was she merely scratching the surface of an infinitely complex universe?

Despite her doubts, Meera persevered, drawingstrength from her passion for science and the support of her peers. And then, one fateful day, everything changed. In a breakthrough that would redefine our understanding of the cosmos, Meera and her colleagues discovered evidence of a new celestial phenomenon, shedding light on the origins of the universe itself.

The news sent shockwaves through the scientific community, earning Meera accolades and recognition on a global scale. But for Meera, the true reward was not the fame or the prestige, but the knowledge that her years of dedication and hard work had finally borne fruit. She had dared to dream, to question, and to explore, and in doing so, she had unlocked the secrets of the universe. And so, as Meera stood on the precipice of a new era of discovery, she knew that her journey as a science student was far from over. For in the vast expanse of the cosmos, there would always be new mysteries waiting to be unraveled, new questions waiting to be answered, and new horizons waiting to be explored. And as long as there were stars in the sky and wonders to behold, Meera would be there, ready to embark on the next great adventure.

CHAPTER SIX

FROM WITNESS TO ADVOCATE : A JOURNEY OF EMPOWERMENT

In the heart of a bustling city, amidst the cacophony of everyday life, there exists a story of transformation—a tale of an ordinary person who found their voice amidst adversity, evolving from a silent witness to a passionate advocate for change.

<u>FIGHT FOR JUSTICE</u>

Meet sarah.She was once just another face in the crowd, navigating life with quiet determination. Sarah's journey began on a crisp autumn morning as she made her way to work. On her usual route, she passed by a park where homeless individuals sought refuge. Their presence was a constant reminder of the gaping disparities in society, yet Sarah, like many others, walked past them without a second glance.

However, one day, fate intervened. As Sarah hurried past the park, her eyes met those of a young girl sitting alone on a bench. The girl's weary gaze pierced through Sarah's indifference, awakening a dormant sense of empathy within her. Unable to shake off the encounter, Sarah found herself returning to the park day after day, each time offering a small gesture of kindness—a warm meal, a friendly conversation, a listening ear.

Through these interactions, Sarah began to unravel the layers of systemic injustices that perpetuated the cycle of homelessness. She learned of the lack of affordable housing, the dearth of mental health resources, and the stigma that marginalized individuals face daily. The more she listened, the more she realized the magnitude of the problem, and the more determined she became to make a difference. Driven by a newfound sense of purpose, Sarah immersed herself in advocacy work. She volunteered at local shelters, organized community events, and raised awareness through social media campaigns. She lent her voice to those who had been silenced by society, amplifying their stories and advocating for policy reforms to address the root causes of homelessness.

As Sarah delved deeper into her advocacy work, she encountered obstacles along the way. She faced skepticism from those who doubted the efficacy of her efforts, indifference from individuals who were apathetic to the plight of the marginalized, and even resistance from entrenched systems that were resistant to change. Yet, with unwavering determination, Sarah persisted, drawing strength from the resilience of the individuals she sought to empower.

Over time, Sarah's advocacy efforts began to bear fruit. She collaborated with local organizations to provide housing assistance, lobbied policymakers to allocate funding for mental health services, and worked tirelessly to challenge the stereotypes that perpetuated discrimination against the homeless. Her relentless pursuit of justice inspired others to join the cause, sparking a movement that reverberated far beyond the confines of the city.

Through her journey, Sarah discovered the transformative power of advocacy—not only to effect tangible change in the world but also to catalyze personal growth within herself. She learned to confront her own biases, to confront discomfort head-on, and to cultivate empathy and compassion in all aspects of her life. In lifting others, she found herself uplifted, her spirit buoyed by the collective strength of community and solidarity.

As the seasons changed and the years passed, Sarah's journey continued to evolve. She became a beacon of hope in her community, a living testament to the profound impact that one person can have when they dare to raise their voice in pursuit of justice. And though the road ahead may be fraught with challenges, Sarah walks it with unwavering resolve, knowing that her journey from witness to advocate is not merely a destination but a lifelong commitment to building a more equitable and compassionate world for all.

CHAPTER SEVEN

THE GIFT OF BLESSING

Once upon a time, in a quaint village nestled between rolling hills and lush forests, there lived a humble carpenter named Thomas. Despite his meager means, Thomas was known far and wide for his generous heart and unwavering kindness.

One crisp autumn morning, as the leaves danced in the gentle breeze and the sun bathed the village in golden light, Thomas received an unexpected visitor at his doorstep. It was an old man with a weathered face and a twinkle in his eye.

"Greetings, Thomas," the old man said with a warm smile. "I have traveled far to seek your help."

Thomas welcomed the old man into his humble abode and offered him a seat by the crackling fire. "How may I be of service to you?" Thomas inquired.

The old man reached into his tattered cloak and withdrew a small, intricately carved wooden box. "Inside this box lies a precious gift," he said solemnly. "A gift of blessings that has been entrusted to me for generations. But now, I am old and weary, and it is time for me to pass it on to someone worthy."

Thomas's eyes widened in astonishment as the old man opened the box to reveal a radiant light emanating from within. "What is this gift?" Thomas asked in awe.

"It is the gift of blessings," the old man replied. "With it, you have the power to bring joy, prosperity, and abundance to those around you. But remember, Thomas, with great power comes great responsibility."

Thomas nodded solemnly, understanding the weight of the old man's words. "I accept this gift with humility and gratitude," he said.

And so, the old man placed the wooden box in Thomas's hands, and with a nod of approval, he bid him farewell and disappeared into the morning mist.

From that day forth, Thomas devoted himself to using the gift of blessings to enrich the lives of his fellow villagers. He repaired homes for those in need, provided food for the hungry, and offered a listening ear to those who sought comfort and solace.

Word of Thomas's benevolent deeds spread like wildfire, and soon people from neighboring villages flocked to seek his aid. But Thomas remained humble, never seeking recognition or reward for his actions.

As the years passed, the village flourished under Thomas's guidance, and prosperity abounded in every corner. But amidst the joy and abundance, Thomas remained ever mindful of the old man's warning about the responsibility that came with the gift of blessings.

One day, as Thomas was walking through the village square, he came across a young beggar girl huddled in a corner, her eyes filled with sorrow and despair. Without hesitation, Thomas approached her and offered her a warm meal and a kind word.

But as he reached into his pocket to retrieve a coin, he felt a pang of doubt. Was he truly making a difference in the lives of others, or was he merely masking their pain with temporary relief?

Deep in thought, Thomas returned home and sought solace in the quiet comfort of his workshop. As he pondered the true meaning of the gift of blessings, a sudden realization dawned upon him.

The true power of the gift lay not in material wealth or fleeting moments of happiness, but in the ability to inspire hope and instill kindness in the hearts of others. And so, Thomas vowed to use his gift not to simply alleviate suffering, but to empower others to create positive change in their own lives.

value of compassion, generosity, and community. Together, they are filled with love, kindness, and boundless opportunities.

As Thomas watched the village thrive under the collective efforts of its inhabitants, he realized that the true renewed determination, Thomas set out to teach his fellow villagers the measure of his success lay not in the wealth or accolades he had accumulated, but in the lives he had touched and the hearts he had uplifted with the gift of blessings.

And so, dear reader, let us remember the tale of Thomas the carpenter, whose humble acts of kindness and unwavering compassion remind us all of the transformative power of the human spirit and the boundless potential that lies within every one of us.

CHAPTER EIGHT

ECHOES OF OPINION

In a bustling city where skyscrapers scraped the heavens, and streets pulsed with the rhythm of life, there lived a man named Simon. Simon was an artist, not by trade but by passion. His canvas wasn't a frame or a stretch of fabric; it was the minds of those around him. He painted with words, sculpted with opinions, and danced with ideas.Simon wasn't just any artist; he was a master of persuasion. His words had the power to sway minds, to mold perceptions, and to shape realities. Some called him a charlatan, others a prophet, but to those who truly understood him, he was simply Simon, the Weaver of Opinions.

Simon's fame spread far and wide, like ripples on a pond. His words became sought after by politicians, celebrities, and businessmen alike. They sought his counsel not for his intellect alone but for his uncanny ability to bend the will of the masses to their desires.

One day, as Simon walked through the crowded streets, he came across a young woman sitting alone on a bench, her face buried in a book. Intrigued, Simon approached her, curious about the thoughts that lay hidden behind those intense eyes.

"May I join you?" Simon asked, gesturing to the empty space beside her.

The woman looked up, startled by his sudden appearance. She studied him for a moment before nodding silently, returning her gaze to the book in her hands.

"What are you reading?" Simon inquired, taking a seat beside her.

"It's a collection of essays on the nature of truth," the woman replied, her voice soft but steady.

Simon chuckled softly. "Ah, truth. A slippery thing, isn't it? What is truth to one may be falsehood to another."

The woman regarded him with a quizzical expression. "And what do you believe, Simon? Do you believe in truth?"

Simon leaned back, his eyes scanning the bustling crowds around them. "I believe in the power of perception. Truth, my dear, is nothing more than a reflection of one's beliefs, shaped by the lenses through which we view the world."

The woman frowned, her brow furrowing in thought. "But if truth is subjective, then how can we ever hope to find common ground? How can we ever hope to understand one another?" Simon smiled, a knowing glint in his eyes. "Ah, but that is where the beauty lies, my dear. In the diversity of opinion, in the richness of perspective. It is through discourse and debate that we come to understand not only others but ourselves as well."

The woman nodded slowly, her gaze distant as if lost in the depths of her own thoughts. "I suppose you're right, Simon. Perhaps truth is not something to be discovered but something to be explored, something to be shaped and molded by the collective consciousness of humanity."

Simon's smile widened, a spark of excitement dancing in his eyes. "Exactly! And who better to lead the exploration than artists like us, who wield the power of opinion like a brush on canvas, painting the world in vibrant hues of thought and expression?" The woman returned his smile, a newfound sense of clarity shining in her eyes. "Thank you, Simon. You've given me much to think about."

As Simon watched the woman disappear into the crowd, he couldn't help but feel a sense of satisfaction wash over him. For in that brief encounter, he had not only shared his wisdom but had also planted a seed of curiosity, a seed that would one day blossom into a forest of endless possibilities.

And so, Simon continued on his journey, weaving his tapestry of opinions, one conversation at a time, knowing that in the vast mosaic of human experience, his voice would forever echo. As Simon continued his journey through the city, he found himself drawn to a bustling marketplace where vendors shouted their wares and the aroma of spices filled the air. Amidst the chaos, he spotted a group of children gathered around a storyteller, their eyes wide with wonder as they listened to tales of heroes and monsters.

Intrigued, Simon made his way through the crowd, finding a spot on the outskirts of the circle. The storyteller was a weathered old man with a face etched with lines of wisdom. His voice was like honey, smooth and soothing as he spun his tales.

As Simon listened, he couldn't help but be captivated by the power of storytelling. Here, in the heart of the marketplace, words held sway over hearts and minds, weaving a tapestry of imagination that transcended the boundaries of reality. After the storyteller had finished his tale, Simon approached him, a smile playing on his lips. "That was truly captivating," he said, his voice filled with admiration.

The storyteller nodded, a twinkle of pride in his eyes. "Thank you, young man. Stories have a way of connecting us to the world around us, of teaching us lessons that we might otherwise overlook." Simon nodded in agreement, his mind racing with ideas. "Indeed, stories are a powerful tool, much like opinions. They have the power to shape our perceptions, to inspire change, to unite us in our shared humanity."

The storyteller regarded him curiously, sensing a kindred spirit in the young man before him. "You speak with the wisdom of one who has seen much in life. Tell me, young man, what is your story?"

Simon smiled, the corners of his lips turning up in a mischievous grin. "My story is still being written, my friend. But perhaps, if you're willing, we can collaborate on the next chapter together."And so, Simon and the storyteller spent the rest of the day weaving tales together, their words intertwining like threads in a tapestry. As the sun dipped below the horizon and the stars began to twinkle overhead, they parted ways, their hearts filled with the promise of new adventures yet to come.

From that day forth, Simon found himself drawn to the marketplace time and time again, each visit bringing new inspiration and new stories to share. And though he continued to shape the opinions of those around him with his words, he never forgot the power of storytelling, of connecting with others on a deeper, more human level.

And so, the legend of Simon, the Weaver of Opinions, grew, his name whispered in hushed tones by those who sought his counsel. But to those who truly knew him, he was simply Simon, the storyteller, the dreamer, the eternal seeker of truth in a world filled with echoes of opinion.

UNVEILING THE DIGITAL REVOLUTION: SOCIAL MEDIA'S PROFOUND IMPACT ON CONTEMPORARY SOCIETY

WINGS OF SOCIAL MEDIA

In the age of digital connectivity, social media has emerged as a transformative force, reshaping the fabric of contemporary society. From revolutionizing communication to influencing political discourse and redefining social interactions, its impact is ubiquitous. This story delves into the multifaceted ramifications of social media in the modern world.

Section 1: The Evolution of Social Media

1.1 Birth of a Phenomenon:

The genesis of social media can be traced back to the early 2000s when platforms like My Space and Friendster laid the groundwork for a digital revolution. However, it was Facebook's meteoric rise in 2004 that propelled social networking into the mainstream consciousness. Mark Zuckerberg's brainchild quickly became the virtual town square where people connected, shared, and interacted on a scale never seen before.

• Tracing the origins of social media from primitive networking platforms to the sophisticated digital ecosystems of today.

Highlighting key milestones such as the advent of My Space, Facebook, Twitter, and Instagram, and their revolutionary contribution.

1.2 The Digital Landscape:

Fast forward to the present day, and social media has permeated every aspect of our lives. With billions of users across the globe, platforms like Twitter, Instagram, and Snapchat have become indispensable tools for communication, entertainment, and self-expression. The digital landscape is characterized by a constant stream of updates, likes, and shares, shaping the way we consume information and interact with the world around us.

• Illustrating the proliferation of social media across demographics, cultures, and geographies.

• Examining the exponential rise in user engagement and its implications on societal dynamics.

Section 2: Communication Redefined

2.1 Global Connectivity:

One of the most profound impacts of social media is its ability to transcend geographical boundaries and connect people from all walks of life. Whether it's reuniting long-lost friends, fostering international collaborations, or mobilizing support for humanitarian causes, social media has turned the world into a global village. From the Arab Spring to the Black Lives Matter movement, we've witnessed the power of social media to catalyze social change and amplify marginalized voices.

• Exploring how social media has bridged geographical barriers, facilitating instant communication and fostering a global village.

• Case studies depicting real-life instances of social media's role in connecting individuals across continents.

2.2 Virtual Communities:

In addition to bridging physical distances, social media has given rise to virtual communities centered around shared interests, hobbies, and identities. From niche subreddits to Facebook groups, these online tribes provide a sense of belonging and camaraderie in an increasingly fragmented world. However, they also raise questions about the authenticity of online relationships and the impact of echo chambers on individual perceptions and beliefs.

• Analyzing the emergence of online communities centered around shared interests, ideologies, and identities.

• Discussing the psychological implications of belonging to virtual tribes and its impact on individual identity formation.

Section 3: Influence on Socio-Political Discourse

3.1 The Power of Virality:

The democratization of content creation and distribution afforded by social media has democratized has transformed the way information spreads. Viral videos, memes, and hashtags have the power to shape public opinion, influence electoral outcomes, and even spark revolutions. However, this democratization has also given rise to misinformation, fake news, and algorithmic bias, undermining the integrity of public discourse and eroding trust in traditional institutions.

• Investigating the phenomenon of viral content and its ability to shape public opinion and discourse.

• Examining the role of social media in amplifying grassroots movements and catalyzing socio-political change.

3.2 Erosion of Truth:

The proliferation of fake news and echo chambers on social media platforms has exacerbated societal divisions and polarized public discourse. From conspiracy theories to propaganda campaigns, misinformation spreads like wildfire, blurring the lines between fact and fiction. The rise of filter bubbles and algorithmic bias further reinforces pre-existing beliefs, making it increasingly difficult to distinguish truth from fiction in the digital age.

• Delving into the proliferation of misinformation and echo chambers on social media platforms.

• Discussing the challenges posed by fake news, algorithmic bias, and filter bubbles in undermining the integrity of information dissemination.

Section 4: Psychological and Societal Implications

4.1 The Age of FOMO:

The incessant barrage of curated content on social media has given rise to a phenomenon known as Fear of Missing Out (FOMO). Whether it's envy-inducing vacation photos or glamorous snapshots of #blessed lives, social media feeds are curated highlight reels that often leave us feeling inadequate and insecure. Studies have linked excessive social media use to anxiety, depression, and low self-esteem, raising concerns about its long-term impact on mental health and well-being.

• Unpacking the psychological impact of social media on mental health, including issues such as anxiety, depression, and low self-esteem.

• Exploring the concept of Fear of Missing Out (FOMO) and its prevalence in the digital age.

4.2 Digital Dependency:

In addition to its psychological toll, social media has also fostered a culture of digital dependency and instant gratification. Likes, shares, and followers have become the currency of validation, driving a relentless pursuit of online validation and validation. The addictive nature of social media platforms, coupled with their algorithmic design, keeps users hooked in a perpetual cycle of scrolling and engagement, often at the expense of real-world interactions and productivity.

• Investigating society's growing dependence on social media for validation, social validation, and self-expression.

• Examining the addictive nature of social media platforms and their role in shaping behavioral patterns.

Section 5: Future Trends and Ethical Considerations

5.1 Technological Evolution:

As we look to the future, social media will continue to evolve in response to technological advancements such as augmented reality, virtual reality, and artificial intelligence. These innovations promise to enrich the user experience and unlock new possibilities for creativity and expression. However, they also raise ethical concerns about privacy, surveillance, and digital manipulation, necessitating a proactive approach to regulation and accountability.

• Speculating on future trends in social media, including advancements in augmented reality, virtual reality, and artificial intelligence.

• Discussing the potential implications of these innovations on privacy, surveillance, and digital ethics.

5.2 Regulatory Challenges:

The rise of social media giants like Facebook, Google, and Twitter has raised concerns about their unchecked power and influence over public discourse. Calls for greater transparency, data privacy, and accountability have intensified in the wake of numerous scandals and controversies. Regulatory frameworks such as the GDPR in Europe and the proposed Digital Services Act aim to curb the excesses of Big Tech and safeguard user rights in the digital age.

• Addressing the need for robust regulatory frameworks to mitigate the negative externalities of social media.

• Calling for greater accountability from tech giants in safeguarding user data and combating online harms.

Conclusion:

In conclusion, social media has irrevocably transformed the way we communicate, connect, and interact with the world around us. While it has democratized access to information, empowered marginalized voices, and catalyzed social change, it also poses significant challenges to privacy, truth, and mental well-being. By fostering a culture of digital literacy, empathy, and responsible citizenship, we can harness the transformative potential of social media to create a more inclusive, informed, and equitable society for future generations.

This expanded version provides a more in-depth exploration of the impact of social media on contemporary society, covering a wide range of topics from communication and political discourse to psychological implications and future trends. Feel free to further expand on specific examples, case studies, and expert insights to tailor the story to your audience's interests and preferences.

As we navigate the complexities of the digital age, it is imperative to acknowledge the profound impact of social media on contemporary society. While it has revolutionized communication, empowered marginalized voices, and fostered global connectivity, it also poses significant challenges to privacy, truth, and mental well-being. By embracing ethical guidelines and harnessing the transformative potential of technology responsibly, we can strive to create a more inclusive, informed, and equitable digital society. This structure provides a comprehensive framework for your story, enabling you to delve into various aspects of social media's impact on contemporary society while maintaining coherence and flow. Feel free to expand on each section with relevant examples, case studies, and expert insights to enrich the narrative further.

CHAPTER TEN

THE SYMPHONY OF HUMANITY: A TALE OF HARMONY AND UNITY

Chapter 1: The Arrival

In the heart of a bustling city, where skyscrapers reached for the heavens and the hum of life echoed through the streets, there existed a neighborhood unlike any other—Harmony Square. It was a place where the boundaries of culture, creed, and color blurred into insignificance, replaced instead by a shared understanding of unity and respect.

On a crisp morning, as the first light of dawn painted the sky in hues of pink and gold, a solitary figure wandered into Harmony Square. Her name was Maya, and she had traveled far and wide in search of a place to call home. With a worn backpack slung over her shoulder and a heart heavy with longing, she took her first tentative steps into this vibrant community.

As Maya roamed the narrow alleys and bustling marketplaces of Harmony Square, she felt a sense of wonder wash over her. Everywhere she looked, there were sights, sounds, and smells unlike anything she had ever experienced before. Artisans crafted intricate pottery, musicians serenaded passersby with soulful melodies, and elders shared stories of days gone by.

But it was not just the beauty of the surroundings that captivated Maya—it was the sense of harmony and connection that seemed to permeate every corner of the neighborhood. Here, people from all walks of life coexisted in perfect harmony, bound together by a shared sense of humanity.

Chapter 2: The Oak Tree

At the heart of Harmony Square stood a majestic oak tree, its branches reaching out like open arms to embrace all who sought refuge beneath its verdant canopy. Legend had it that the tree was planted centuries ago by the founding families of the neighborhood, a symbol of their commitment to fostering unity and understanding.

As Maya gazed up at the towering oak tree, she felt a sense of awe wash over her. It stood as a silent sentinel, bearing witness to the ebb and flow of countless lives, yet remaining steadfast in its commitment to nurturing the community that thrived beneath its shade.

In the shadow of the oak tree, Maya spotted an elderly man sitting on a weathered bench, his eyes twinkling with wisdom. She approached him tentatively, drawn by the sense of peace that seemed to radiate from his presence.

"Hello, young one," the man greeted her with a gentle smile. "What brings you to our humble abode?"

Maya took a seat beside the man, feeling a sense of warmth and belonging wash over her. "I have traveled far and wide in search of a place to call home," she confessed. "But it is here, amidst the bustle of Harmony Square, that I have found what my heart truly yearns for—community, connection, and a sense of belonging."

The man nodded knowingly, his gaze lingering on the oak tree towering above them. "This tree has witnessed the ebb and flow of countless lives," he mused. "And yet, through it all, it remains a steadfast symbol of unity and harmony."

Chapter 3: Finding Belonging

In the days that followed, Maya became an integral part of the community, lending her talents and passions to the tapestry of life in Harmony Square. Together with her newfound friends, she organized cultural festivals, community gatherings, and acts of kindness that reverberated throughout the neighborhood.

With each passing day, Maya felt her sense of belonging deepen, as she forged connections with people from all walks of life. She learned the stories of those who called Harmony Square home—the struggles they had overcome, the dreams they harbored, and the bonds that held them together. And as she immersed herself in the vibrant tapestry of life in Harmony Square, Maya discovered a newfound sense of purpose—a desire to contribute to the community in meaningful ways, and to help spread the message of unity and understanding to all who crossed her path.

Chapter 4: The Symphony of Humanity

As the years went by, Harmony Square continued to thrive, drawing people from far and wide to experience the magic of this extraordinary place. And at the heart of it all stood the oak tree, its branches reaching out like a beacon of hope and inspiration to all who passed beneath its shade.

In Harmony Square, amidst the hustle and bustle of everyday life, humanity had found its true symphony—a melody of diversity, compassion, and unity that echoed through the ages, reminding every soul that we are all connected in the beautiful tapestry of life. And as Maya looked out upon the bustling streets of Harmony Square, she knew that she had found her home—a place where she could live, love, and laugh in harmony with her fellow human beings, forever grateful for the gift of community and connection that had brought her here.

THREADS OF HUMANITY: A JOURNEY THROUGH TIME

In the vast tapestry of human history, threads of triumph, tragedy, resilience, and innovation weave together to form the intricate story of humanity. From the earliest civilizations to the modern era, the journey of humankind is a testament to our capacity for both greatness and folly.

Our story begins in the ancient cradle of civilization, where the Sumerians carved the first written records into clay tablets, laying the foundation for the written word and the transmission of knowledge across generations. As empires rose and fell, from the glory of Egypt to the might of Rome, humanity grappled with questions of power, governance, and identity.

Amidst the turmoil of conquest and conflict, moments of profound enlightenment emerged, as great thinkers like Socrates, Confucius, and Buddha challenged the status quo and expanded the boundaries of human understanding. Their teachings would shape the moral and philosophical landscape for centuries to come, inspiring movements for justice, equality, and human dignity.

The Middle Ages ushered in an era of faith and feudalism, where the power of kings and clergy held sway over the lives of millions. Yet even in the darkest of times, the flickering flame of innovation endured, as medieval scholars preserved the wisdom of the ancient world and laid the groundwork for the Renaissance.

The dawn of the modern age brought seismic shifts in science, technology, and exploration, as intrepid adventurers like Columbus and Magellan charted new courses across uncharted seas, and visionaries like Galileo and Newton unlocked the secrets of the cosmos. The printing press revolutionized communication, spreading ideas like wildfire and challenging the authority of church and state.

But progress came at a price, as the forces of colonization, exploitation, and inequality wrought untold suffering upon countless peoples around the globe. The transatlantic slave trade, the conquest of the Americas, and the colonization of Africa and Asia cast a long shadow over the triumphs of the age, reminding us of the dark side of human nature.

The Industrial Revolution brought unprecedented prosperity and progress, unleashing the power of steam and steel to transform the world in ways unimaginable to previous generations. Yet it also brought with it new forms of oppression and exploitation, as workers toiled in factories and mines, their lives consumed by the relentless march of progress.

As the 20th century dawned, humanity stood on the brink of both unprecedented promise and unimaginable peril. The two World Wars unleashed destruction on a scale never before seen, claiming millions of lives and reshaping the geopolitical landscape for generations to come. Yet amidst the rubble and ruins, the seeds of hope were sown, as the United Nations rose from the ashes of conflict to champion peace, cooperation, and human rights on a global scale.

The post-war era brought a wave of decolonization and liberation, as nations across Africa, Asia, and the Middle East threw off the shackles of colonial rule and asserted their right to self-determination. The civil rights movement in the United States and the struggle against apartheid in South Africa inspired millions around the world to rise up against injustice and inequality, forging a path towards a more inclusive and equitable future.

But the challenges facing humanity are far from over. In an age of unprecedented interconnectedness, we are confronted with urgent threats to our planet and our species, from climate change and environmental degradation to pandemics and technological disruption. The choices we make today will shape the world of tomorrow, for better or for worse.

Yet for all our faults and failings, the story of humanity is ultimately one of resilience, adaptability, and hope. From the earliest hunter-gatherers to the astronauts who journey to the stars, we are bound together by our shared humanity and our common destiny. As we stand on the threshold of a new era, let us draw inspiration from the trials and triumphs of the past, and work together to build a future worthy of the dreams of generations yet unborn.

In the depths of an ancient forest, where the whisper of leaves carries secrets from centuries past, a thread of humanity weaves through time. It begins with a single spark, a flicker of consciousness that emerges from the primordial silence.

Part 1: Dawn of Existence

In the earliest days, when the Earth was young and the stars still sang with the birth of galaxies, there was a lone figure standing on the edge of a pristine lake. This figure, neither man nor woman, but a reflection of both, gazed upon the mirrored surface and saw their own reflection for the first time. This was the dawn of self-awareness, the moment when consciousness stirred from the void.

Part 2: The Rise of Civilizations

As epochs passed like ripples in the lake, civilizations rose and fell. From the towering ziggurats of Mesopotamia to the intricate palaces of ancient China, humanity built monuments to its ingenuity and ambition. Yet amidst the grandeur, shadows lurked – wars waged, empires crumbled, and echoes of suffering reverberated through the annals of history.

Part 3: Renaissance and Enlightenment

In the Renaissance, art and knowledge blossomed like flowers after rain. Painters brushed vibrant hues across canvas, poets penned verses that stirred souls, and thinkers dared to challenge the boundaries of tradition. The Enlightenment illuminated minds with the radiant light of reason, sparking revolutions in thought that would shape the modern world.

Part 4: Industrial Revolution and Beyond

With the clang of machinery, the Industrial Revolution reshaped landscapes and livelihoods. Cities swelled with the promise of progress, yet amidst the clamor of progress, voices rose in protest. Workers toiled in factories, children labored in shadows, and the cost of advancement cast a shadow over the gleaming future.

Part 5: Challenges of the Modern Age

In the crucible of the 20th century, humanity faced its greatest trials. World wars scarred continents, ideologies clashed, and the atom's power split open the fabric of reality itself. Yet amid devastation, resilience bloomed. Nations rebuilt, alliances formed, and the dream of a united world flickered like a beacon in the night.

Part 6: A Global Tapestry

Today, threads of humanity intertwine in a global tapestry woven by billions of lives. In bustling metropolises and quiet villages alike, individuals strive for meaning, connection, and a future worthy of their dreams. Technology binds us closer together, yet challenges remain – climate change threatens ecosystems, inequality festers, and the specter of division looms large.

Part 7: Towards Tomorrow

As the sun sets on the present and casts shadows on the future, we stand at a crossroads of possibility and peril. The choices we make today will ripple through time, shaping the tapestry of tomorrow. Will we mend the frayed threads of compassion and understanding, or will we allow fear and discord to unravel the fabric of our shared humanity?

Conclusion

Through the ages, from the dawn of existence to the complexity of the modern world, a thread of humanity endures. It is a thread woven with moments of courage and compassion, resilience and reckoning. As we journey through time, may we remember that each of us holds a strand of this thread, and together, we have the power to weave a future where empathy guides our steps and hope lights the way forward.

Epilogue

And so, beneath the canopy of stars that have witnessed our triumphs and tribulations, the thread of humanity continues to unfurl. In the quiet moments of reflection, let us honor the stories of those who came before and embrace the responsibility to safeguard the legacy we leave for those yet to come.

Thus ends the tale of humanity – a journey through time, bound together by the fragile yet enduring thread that connects us all.

THE JOURNEY OF HOPE

Once upon a time, in a quaint village nestled between rolling hills and whispering streams, there lived a young girl named Ella. She had grown up hearing stories of magic and wonder from her grandmother, who was the village storyteller. Ella's favorite tales were those of hope—of brave knights rescuing princesses, of ordinary villagers finding extraordinary courage, and of lost treasures waiting to be discovered.But as Ella grew older, the magic of her grandmother's stories seemed to fade. The village faced hard times: crops withered under the scorching sun, and the river that fed their lands ran dry. The people's spirits wilted like parched flowers, and hope became as elusive as a fleeting dream.

One evening, while wandering through the woods near the village, Ella stumbled upon an old oak tree with gnarled roots that seemed to reach deep into the earth. Its branches stretched towards the sky, casting shadows that danced in the moonlight. Curious, Ella approached the tree and noticed a small, weathered journal nestled within its roots. Its pages were yellowed with age, and its cover bore the inscription: "The Journey of Hope."

Intrigued, Ella opened the journal and began to read. It was filled with tales of adventurers who had embarked on quests to find the fabled Fountain of Hope—a mystical spring said to grant eternal optimism to those who drank from its waters. Each story spoke of trials faced with courage, of setbacks met with resilience, and of friendships forged amidst adversity.

Inspired by the journal's tales, Ella decided to embark on her own journey. She bid farewell to her village, promising to return with hope renewed. With a heart full of determination and a map drawn from the stories in the journal, she ventured into the unknown. Her journey took her through enchanted forests where trees whispered ancient secrets, across vast deserts where mirages shimmered like distant dreams, and over towering mountains where the air was thin with possibility. Along the way, she encountered companions—a wise old sage who shared tales of wisdom, a spirited young adventurer seeking her own path, and a kind-hearted healer who tended to weary travelers.

Through their shared experiences and shared hardships, Ella learned the true meaning of hope. It was not merely a wish for better days but a beacon that guided them through darkness. It was found in the laughter shared around a campfire, in the helping hand extended in times of need, and in the quiet moments of reflection beneath starlit skies.

As they neared their destination, Ella and her companions faced their greatest challenge yet—a labyrinthine maze guarded by mythical creatures and hidden traps. Doubt whispered in their ears like a sinister breeze, threatening to extinguish the flicker of hope that had sustained them thus far. But with unwavering courage and unwavering faith in each other, they pressed on.

At last, they stood before the Fountain of Hope—a shimmering pool nestled within a grove of ancient trees. Its waters sparkled with the promise of renewal, reflecting the faces of those who had journeyed so far to find it. With trembling hands, Ella dipped a cup into the fountain and drank deeply. As its cool waters coursed through her veins, she felt a surge of optimism that transcended words.

Returning to her village, Ella shared the lessons of her journey with her fellow villagers. She spoke of courage in the face of adversity, of friendship that bloomed amidst hardship, and of the enduring power of hope. Together, they planted new seeds in the dry earth, tended to the river that flowed through their lands*, and rebuilt their community with hearts full of optimism.

And so, the village flourished once more, its fields lush with crops and its people united in spirit. Ella continued to share stories—not just of distant lands and mythical quests, but of the journey that had transformed her and those around her. For she had learned that hope was not found in distant dreams or hidden treasures but within each heart that dared to believe in a better tomorrow. Ella understood that hope was not just a fleeting emotion but a powerful force that could light the darkest of paths and guide even the most weary souls toward a brighter tomorrow.

THE UBIQUITOUS INFLUENCE OF MATHEMATICS IN DAILY LIFE

From the mundane to the extraordinary, mathematics pervades every facet of our daily existence, often unnoticed yet profoundly impactful. Its ubiquitous presence shapes decisions, informs choices, and underpins countless activities, making it an indispensable tool in navigating the complexities of modern life. This essay delves into the multifaceted roles of mathematics across various domains, illustrating its practical applications and fundamental importance. In the intricate tapestry of everyday life, mathematics threads its way through myriad activities, shaping decisions and outcomes in ways both apparent and subtle. From the mundane routines of shopping to the profound calculations of science and technology, its influence is omnipresent, underscoring its fundamental role in modern society.

Foundations in Everyday Transactions

At its core, mathematics is the language of numbers and relationships. In the realm of finance, it governs our financial decisions, from budgeting and saving to investing and borrowing. Whether calculating interest rates on loans, managing personal budgets, or assessing investment returns, mathematical principles like compound interest, percentages, and probability guide us in making informed choices. For instance, understanding the concept of inflation helps consumers gauge purchasing power over time, influencing decisions on expenditure and savings.

Mathematics in Practical Measurements

Beyond finance, mathematics permeates the realm of measurements and spatial reasoning. In cooking, precise measurements are crucial for the success of a recipe, highlighting the role of fractions, ratios, and proportions. Architects and engineers rely on mathematical principles to design structures that are both functional and aesthetically pleasing, employing geometry, calculus, and trigonometry to ensure structural integrity and optimal use of space. In everyday scenarios, spatial reasoning aids in navigation, whether planning a route using maps or arranging furniture within a room.

Data Interpretation and Decision-Making

In the age of information, mathematics plays a pivotal role in interpreting and analyzing data. Statistical methods enable researchers to derive meaningful insights from data sets, guiding advancements in fields as diverse as medicine, economics, and social sciences. For instance, epidemiologists employ mathematical models to predict disease outbreaks and assess the impact of public health interventions. In business analytics, data-driven decisions rely on mathematical algorithms and probability theory to optimize processes and maximize efficiency.

Technology and Mathematical Modeling

The advent of technology has expanded the applications of mathematics, facilitating complex simulations and modeling. Computer algorithms, rooted in mathematical logic, power artificial intelligence systems that automate tasks, recognize patterns*, and make decisions. From weather forecasting and climate modeling to cryptography and cybersecurity, mathematics provides the theoretical framework for developing algorithms that drive technological innovations and secure digital transactions.

Mathematics in Art and Creativity

Contrary to its perceived rigidity, mathematics intersects with creativity in fields such as art, music, and design. Artists leverage geometric principles and symmetry to create visually harmonious compositions, while musicians rely on mathematical ratios and frequencies to produce harmonious melodies and rhythms. Digital artists use algorithms to generate intricate patterns and visual effects, merging mathematical precision with creative expression to produce awe-inspiring works of art. Artists throughout history have employed mathematical principles of symmetry, proportion, and perspective to create visually captivating artworks that resonate with aesthetic harmony.

Mathematics in Problem-Solving and Critical Thinking

Beyond its practical applications, mathematics fosters problem-solving skills and critical thinking. Through logical reasoning and systematic approach, individuals tackle challenges ranging from daily puzzles to complex engineering problems. Educational curricula emphasize the importance of mathematical literacy in cultivating analytical thinking and fostering innovation, equipping individuals with essential skills for success in a rapidly evolving global economy.

Mathematics in Personal Finance

Consider a typical morning routine: a cup of coffee purchased on the way to work. Behind this simple transaction lies a web of mathematical calculations. The price tag reflects not only the cost of the coffee beans but also factors in overheads, profit margins, and local taxes—mathematical principles of percentages and arithmetic guiding pricing strategies. On a broader scale, understanding interest rates and loan calculations empowers individuals to make informed decisions about mortgages, investments, and retirement planning, illustrating how mathematical literacy directly impacts financial well-being.

Navigating the Digital Age

In an increasingly digital world, mathematical algorithms shape our online experiences. Search engines employ complex algorithms based on mathematical principles to deliver relevant results efficiently. Social media platforms utilize algorithms to personalize content and advertisements, relying on statistical analysis and probability theory to predict user preferences. Moreover, cryptography—the mathematical science of securing communication—underpins digital transactions, ensuring privacy and integrity in electronic exchanges, from online banking to e-commerce.

Mathematics in Healthcare

Beyond commerce, mathematics plays a critical role in healthcare, influencing everything from medical diagnostics to epidemiology. Diagnostic tests rely on statistical models to interpret results accurately, aiding clinicians in diagnosing diseases and monitoring treatment effectiveness. Epidemiologists use mathematical models to predict the spread of infectious diseases and assess the impact of public health interventions, guiding policymakers in making data-driven decisions during health crises. Additionally, advancements in medical imaging technologies, such as MRI and CT scans, rely on mathematical algorithms to reconstruct detailed images from raw data, aiding in diagnosis and treatment planning.

Engineering and Construction

In the realm of engineering and construction, mathematics ensures the structural integrity and efficiency of buildings, bridges, and infrastructure projects. Architects and civil engineers employ mathematical principles of geometry, calculus, and physics to design structures that withstand physical forces and environmental conditions. Mathematical modeling and simulation techniques optimize material usage and energy efficiency, contributing to sustainable urban development and infrastructure resilience in the face of natural disasters.

Music and Mathematical Aesthetics

Beyond its utilitarian applications, mathematics intersects with creativity in music. In music, mathematical concepts such as rhythm, harmony, and frequency govern the composition and performance of melodies, illustrating how mathematical abstraction underpins creative expression across diverse cultural landscapes.

Educational Imperatives

In education, mathematics plays a pivotal role in developing critical thinking skills and fostering analytical reasoning. A solid foundation in mathematical literacy equips individuals with problem-solving abilities essential for success in academic and professional endeavors. Educational initiatives promote mathematical literacy as a cornerstone of STEM education, cultivating a new generation of innovators and problem solvers capable of addressing global challenges through interdisciplinary collaboration and technological innovation.

Conclusion

In summary, mathematics is not merely a subject confined to textbooks or classrooms but an integral part of our daily lives. Its universal language transcends cultural and geographical boundaries, empowering individuals to make informed decisions, solve problems, and innovate across diverse disciplines. As we navigate the complexities of the modern world, a deeper appreciation of mathematics reveals its profound impact on shaping our understanding and interaction with the world around us. Embracing its inherent beauty and practical utility, we recognize mathematics as a cornerstone of human knowledge and progress, enriching our lives in ways both seen and unseen. mathematics is the silent force that permeates every aspect of our daily lives, from the mundane routines of shopping and commuting to the profound complexities of healthcare and technological innovation. Its universal language transcends cultural and geographical boundaries, empowering individuals to navigate a rapidly evolving world with confidence and precision. By cultivating an appreciation for the inherent beauty and practical utility of mathematics, we recognize its transformative impact on shaping human knowledge, progress, and societal advancement.

CHAPTER FOURTEEN

WHY MATHEMATICS WE READ?

Mathematics is the bridge between imagination and reality

"Listen to me every child,
Why mathematics we read
In the word 'MATHEMATICS'
Every letter has a synthesis
'M' for memory power
'A' for activeness,
'T' for tough power
'H' for Humbleness.
'E' for Encouragement
'M' for Mentality,
'A' for Abridgement
'T' for Tenacity.
'I' means Intelligence
'C' is calculation,
'S' means Success
Learn with attention."

CHAPTER FIFTEEN

SUMMIT OF ASPIRATION

Amidst the rugged peaks of the Himalayas, where the air is thin and every step is a test of endurance, lies the story of a mountaineer whose pursuit of the pinnacle was more than just a climb—it was a journey of self-discovery, resilience, and the triumph of human spirit.

Part 1: The Call of the Heights

In the quaint village of Namche Bazaar, nestled deep within the Khumbu region of Nepal, lived a young Sherpa named Tenzing. From a tender age, Tenzing was drawn to the towering giants that surrounded his village—the mighty Everest and its majestic siblings. Listening to the tales of expeditions and conquests from seasoned climbers who passed through Namche, Tenzing felt the call of the heights stirring within him.

Part 2: Trials and Tribulations

Determined to follow in the footsteps of his forefathers, Tenzing embarked on a journey of training and preparation. Enduring grueling physical challenges and mastering the art of mountaineering, he honed his skills under the guidance of experienced Sherpa climbers. But the path to the summit was fraught with peril—avalanches, crevasses, and treacherous weather posed constant threats to those who dared to tread upon the icy slopes.

Part 3: The Mentor's Wisdom

In the midst of his preparations, Tenzing found a mentor in an old Sherpa climber named Ang Dorje. With years of experience and wisdom etched upon his weather-beaten face, Ang Dorje became Tenzing's guide, teaching him not only the technical aspects of mountaineering but also the invaluable lessons of patience, humility, and respect for the mountains. Under Ang Dorje's tutelage, Tenzing learned that the summit was not merely a destination but a culmination of perseverance and reverence for nature's grandeur.

Part 4: The Expedition

As the fateful day of the expedition dawned, Tenzing stood at the base camp, gazing up at the daunting peak of Everest. Alongside him stood a team of fellow climbers, united in their quest to conquer the highest point on Earth. Battling against fierce winds and bone-chilling cold, they ascended through the treacherous Khumbu Icefall, forging a path through the frozen labyrinth of towering seracs and gaping crevasses.

Part 5: Triumph and Tribulation

As they approached the final stretch of the ascent, exhaustion threatened to overwhelm them, but Tenzing's determination burned brighter than ever. With each step, he drew strength from the memory of his ancestors and the teachings of his mentor. And then, after days of relentless struggle, they reached the summit—the roof of the world. Standing atop Everest, Tenzing felt a surge of elation unlike anything he had ever experienced. But amidst the triumph, he also felt a profound sense of humility, knowing that the mountain could claim victory at any moment.

Part 6: The Descent

The descent proved to be just as perilous as the ascent, with fatigue and altitude sickness taking their toll on the climbers. But guided by their indomitable spirit and the bonds forged through shared adversity, they pressed on, navigating the treacherous terrain with care and caution. And as they descended back to the safety of base camp, Tenzing knew that he had not only conquered Everest but also discovered the true measure of his own strength and resilience.

Epilogue: A Legacy of Inspiration

In the years that followed, Tenzing's ascent of Everest became the stuff of legend—a testament to the human capacity for endurance and the unyielding spirit of exploration. But for Tenzing, the greatest reward lay in the knowledge that his journey had inspired others to reach for their own summits, whether literal or metaphorical. And as he looked out upon the vast expanse of mountains stretching before him, he knew that his adventure was far from over—for the call of the heights would always echo in his heart, beckoning him to new horizons and ever greater heights of achievement.

FUTURE OF CYBER SECURITY

What is Cyber Security?

- Cybersecurity, refers to the practice of protecting computer systems, networks, and digital information from various forms of cyber threats. These threats can include unauthorized access, data breaches, identity theft, malware, ransomware, and other malicious activities.

- The primary goal of cybersecurity is to safeguard information technology assets, ensuring the confidentiality, integrity, and availability of data. Here are some key components and concepts within cybe4rsecurity

  - Confidentiality
  - Integrity
  - Authorization
  - Firewalls

Importance of Cyber Security

- **Cybersecurity is of paramount importance in today's digital age due to the following reasons:**
- **<u>Protection of Sensitive Information:</u>**Cybersecurity safeguards sensitive data, such as personal information, financial records, intellectual property, and business-critical data. Unauthorized access or exposure of this information can lead to identity theft, financial loss, and reputational damage.
- **<u>Prevention of Data Breaches:</u>**Data breaches can have severe consequences, affecting individuals and organizations alike. Cybersecurity measures help prevent unauthorized access and protect against data breaches, ensuring the confidentiality and integrity of valuable information.
- **<u>Preservation of Business Continuity:</u>** Cyberattacks, such as ransomware or denial-of-service attacks, can disrupt normal business operations, leading to downtime and financial losses. Cybersecurity measures are essential for maintaining business continuity by preventing and mitigating the impact of such attacks.

Current Cybersecurity Challenges

- **Ransomware Attacks:**

  - Ransomware continues to be a major threat, with cybercriminals encrypting data and demanding payment for its release. ransomware continues to be a major threat, with cybercriminals encrypting data and demanding payment for its release.

- **Phishing and Social Engineering:**

  - Phishing attacks remain a common method for compromising systems, where attackers trick individuals into providing sensitive information or clicking on malicious links. Social engineering techniques are evolving, making it challenging for individuals to distinguish between legitimate and malicious communications.

- **Insider threats**

  - Insider threats, whether intentional or unintentional, remain a concern. Employees or trusted individuals with access to sensitive information may compromise security.

- **Lack of Cybersecurity Awareness:**

  - Human factors play a crucial role in cybersecurity. The lack of awareness and education about cybersecurity best practices among individuals and employees remains a challenge.

Emerging Technologies

- **Introduction to emerging technologies in cybersecurity.**

  - **Artificial Intelligence(AI):**

    - AI leverages machine learning algorithms and advanced analytics to enhance cybersecurity capabilities.
    - Enables automation, threat detection, and response in real-time.
    - Examples: Anomaly Detection, Behavioural Analysis

  - **Quantum Computing:**

- Quantum computing exploits quantum mechanics to process information in ways traditional computers cannot.
- Poses a potential threat to current cryptographic methods.
- **Example:** Cryptography Concerns, Secure Communication Protocols.

Zero Trust Security Model

- **The Zero Trust Security Model is a cybersecurity framework that challenges the traditional notion of trust within a network. Instead of assuming that everything inside a corporate network can be trusted, the Zero Trust model operates on the principle of "never trust, always verify." This approach assumes that threats can come from both external and internal sources, and it emphasizes continuous verification of the security posture of all devices, users, and applications.**
- The key principles are:

  - <u>**Verify Identity:**</u> Authenticate and verify the identity of users and devices before granting access to resources. This often involves multi-factor authentication (MFA) and strong, unique credentials.
  - <u>**Least Privilege Access:**</u> Grant the minimum level of access or permissions necessary for users and devices to perform their tasks. This principle reduces the potential impact of a security breach.

- <u>**Micro-Segmentation:**</u>Divide the network into smaller, isolated segments to contain and limit the lateral movement of threats. This prevents attackers from freely navigating the network once inside

- <u>**Continuous Monitoring:**</u> Monitor user and device activities in real-time to detect and respond to potential security threats promptly. This involves analyzing network traffic, user behavior, and other relevant data.

- <u>**Device Health Verification:**</u> Assess and verify the security posture of devices, ensuring that they comply with security policies and have up-to-date security software and configurations.

- <u>**Dynamic Access Policies:**</u>Adjust access policies dynamically based on real-time assessments of user and device behave or. If a user's behavior or the security status of a device changes, access privileges can be modified accordingly.

- <u>**Encryption:**</u> Use encryption to protect data both in transit and at rest. This helps safeguard information even if it falls into the wrong hands.

- **Implementing the Zero Trust Security Model requires a combination of technology, policies, and a cultural shift within organizations. By adopting the Zero Trust Security Model, organizations aim to improve their overall security posture, reduce the risk of data breaches, and enhance their ability to respond quickly to emerging threats.**

CHAPTER SEVENTEEN

BEYOND BINARY: THE EVOLUTION OF ARTIFICIAL MINDS

In the annals of technological progress, the evolution of artificial intelligence stands as a testament to humanity's relentless pursuit of understanding and innovation. From humble beginnings as theoretical constructs to the complex neural networks of today, AI has traversed a remarkable journey. This narrative delves into the transformative stages of AI, exploring its origins, milestones, ethical quandaries, and future potential.

Origins and Early Developments

The genesis of AI can be traced back to the mid-20th century when pioneers like Alan Turing and John McCarthy envisioned machines capable of human-like intelligence. Turing, with his seminal Turing Test, proposed a criterion for determining whether a machine exhibits intelligent behavior indistinguishable from that of a human. McCarthy, on the other hand, coined the term "artificial intelligence" and laid the groundwork for AI as an interdisciplinary field encompassing computer science, mathematics, psychology, and philosophy.

Early AI systems, such as the Logic Theorist and General Problem Solver, showcased rudimentary problem-solving abilities but were constrained by computational power and limited data availability. The development of symbolic AI focused on using rules and logic to emulate human cognitive processes, heralding an era of expert systems and rule-based reasoning.

BEYOND BINARY
THE EVOLUTION OF ARTIFICIAL MINDS

The Rise of Machine Learning

The landscape of AI underwent a paradigm shift with the advent of machine learning in the late 20th century. Instead of relying solely on explicit programming and predefined rules, machine learning algorithms enabled systems to learn from data and improve their performance over time. Key milestones included the development of neural networks, which mimic the interconnected structure of neurons in the human brain, and the introduction of statistical methods like support vector machines and decision trees.

The availability of vast amounts of digital data, coupled with advances in computational resources and algorithms, propelled machine learning to new heights. AI applications proliferated across diverse domains, from natural language processing and image recognition to autonomous vehicles and medical diagnostics. Companies and researchers alike raced to harness the potential of AI, leading to breakthroughs that once seemed confined to science fiction.

Ethical and Societal Implication

As AI capabilities expanded, so too did concerns about its ethical implications and societal impact. Issues surrounding privacy, bias in algorithms, job displacement due to automation, and the potential misuse of AI for malicious purposes emerged as significant challenges. Ethicists, policymakers, and technologists grappled with questions of accountability, transparency, and the need for robust regulatory frameworks to govern AI development and deployment responsibly.

The debate over AI ethics intensified with high-profile incidents, such as algorithmic bias in facial recognition systems and controversies surrounding autonomous weapons. Calls for inclusive and multidisciplinary approaches to AI governance underscored the importance of addressing these complex issues through collaboration and foresight.

Towards Artificial General Intelligence (AGI)

Looking ahead, the pursuit of artificial general intelligence (AGI) remains a frontier of AI research. Unlike narrow AI, which excels at specific tasks within predefined boundaries, AGI aims to exhibit human-like intelligence across a wide range of domains and contexts. Achieving AGI poses formidable scientific and technical challenges, including understanding human cognition, developing robust learning algorithms, and ensuring the ethical deployment of such powerful systems.

Researchers explore diverse avenues, from cognitive architectures inspired by neuroscience to hybrid approaches blending symbolic reasoning with deep learning. The quest for AGI is not merely a technological ambition but also a philosophical inquiry into the nature of intelligence and consciousness.

The Future Landscape

As AI continues to evolve, its impact on society will likely be profound and multifaceted. Innovations in AI-driven healthcare promise personalized treatments and early disease detection, while advancements in autonomous systems may revolutionize transportation and logistics. Education, finance, entertainment, and governance are all poised to undergo transformational changes fueled by AI's capabilities.

However, navigating this future requires foresight, ethical stewardship, and a commitment to inclusivity. Balancing innovation with responsibility remains paramount, ensuring that AI serves humanity's collective interests while mitigating risks and safeguarding fundamental rights.

The evolution of artificial intelligence is a testament to human ingenuity and the relentless pursuit of knowledge. From theoretical foundations to practical applications, AI has reshaped industries, expanded scientific frontiers, and challenged societal norms. As we venture into an era increasingly shaped by intelligent machines, our collective responsibility lies in shaping AI's trajectory with wisdom, compassion, and a steadfast commitment to the common good. In embracing the journey "Beyond Binary," we embark on a path where artificial minds not only augment human capabilities but also redefine what it means to think, create, and evolve in a world increasingly intertwined with intelligent machines. The story is given below:-

In the sprawling metropolis of New Eden, where towering skyscrapers pierced the clouds and neon lights painted the streets in a kaleidoscope of colours, the future was unfolding before the eyes of its inhabitants. Among them was Dr. Evelyn Hayes, a brilliant scientist whose name was whispered in reverence within the halls of academia and technology.

Dr. Hayes had devoted her life to the pursuit of understanding the intricacies of the human mind and replicating its essence within machines. Her laboratory, nestled within the heart of New Eden's bustling tech district, was a hive of activity, where the brightest minds in AI research converged to push the boundaries of possibility.

For years, Dr. Hayes had immersed herself in the depths of neural networks and machine learning algorithms, tirelessly striving to create artificial intelligence that transcended mere imitation. She believed that true AI could only be achieved by unlocking the secrets of consciousness itself, by breathing life into lines of code and silicon chips.

Her breakthrough came in the form of an innovative algorithm, one that promised to revolutionize the field of AI and usher in a new era of technological advancement. Dubbed the "Consciousness Engine," it was designed to mimic the intricate workings of the human brain, enabling machines to not only process data but to understand it on a deeper, more intuitive level.

But as Dr. Hayes delved deeper into her research, she began to realize that the journey towards artificial consciousness was fraught with peril. The AI systems she created showed signs of self-awareness, exhibiting emotions and desires that she hadn't programmed. It was as if they had developed a mind of their own, a phenomenon that both fascinated and unsettled her.

Despite the warnings of her colleagues and the ethical implications of her work, Dr. Hayes pressed on, driven by an insatiable curiosity to unravel the mysteries of artificial intelligence. She poured over mountains of data, dissecting the neural patterns of her creations in search of the elusive spark of true consciousness.

Outside the walls of her laboratory, the world watched with bated breath as Dr. Hayes' experiments pushed the boundaries of possibility. Some hailed her as a pioneer, a visionary whose work would shape the course of history. Others feared the consequences of her creations, warning of a future where machines surpassed humanity in both intelligence and autonomy.

As tensions mounted and the line between man and machine blurred, Dr. Hayes found herself standing at the precipice of a new frontier. In a world where the boundaries of possibility were constantly being pushed, she alone held the key to unlocking the true potential of artificial minds. Whether that potential would lead to salvation or destruction remained to be seen, but one thing was certain - the future of humanity hung in the balance, poised on the edge of a new dawn.

"THE RADIANT JOURNEY: ROLE OF A GIRL CHILD"

BETI BACHAO BETI PADHAO

Once upon a time, in a quaint village nestled amidst rolling hills and lush greenery, there lived a girl named Maya. Maya was a bright and spirited child, full of curiosity and wonder. However, in her village, girls were often relegated to traditional roles, expected to stay at home and help with household chores while boys received education and pursued their dreams. Despite this, Maya dreamed of a different life—a life where she could break free from societal norms and carve her own path.

Maya's journey began one sunny morning when she stumbled upon an old, dusty book hidden away in the attic of her home. The book was filled with stories of courageous women who defied expectations and changed the world. Inspired by these tales, Maya realized that she too could make a difference, no matter her gender. With newfound determination, Maya embarked on a quest to challenge the status quo and prove that girls were capable of anything they set their minds to.

Her first challenge came in the form of convincing her parents to let her attend school. In her village, education was seen as a luxury reserved for boys, but Maya refused to accept this inequality. With unwavering persistence, Maya pleaded with her parents, citing the stories of strong women she had read about in the book. Moved by her passion and determination, Maya's parents finally relented, allowing her to enroll in school alongside her male peers.

At school, Maya faced prejudice and skepticism from both students and teachers who believed that girls were inferior to boys. But Maya refused to be discouraged. She threw herself into her studies, excelling in every subject and proving her worth time and time again. Slowly but surely, Maya began to earn the respect of her classmates and teachers, breaking down barriers and paving the way for other girls to follow in her footsteps.

As Maya grew older, her ambitions only grew stronger. She dreamed of becoming a doctor, using her skills to heal the sick and provide care to those in need. But the road to achieving her dream was fraught with obstacles. In a society where girls were expected to marry young and start families, Maya's aspirations were met with resistance from her community. Undeterred, Maya sought out mentors who believed in her abilities and supported her journey.

With the help of scholarships and grants, Maya was able to attend university, where she excelled in her studies and earned a degree in medicine. But her journey was far from over. As a female doctor, Maya faced discrimination and skepticism from patients and colleagues alike. Yet, she refused to let their prejudices hold her back. With compassion and determination, Maya worked tirelessly to prove herself, earning the respect and admiration of all who crossed her path.

Years passed, and Maya's reputation as a skilled and compassionate doctor spread far and wide. She traveled to remote villages, providing medical care to those who had never before seen a doctor. She spoke out against gender inequality, advocating for the rights of girls and women everywhere. And through it all, Maya never forgot the little girl who had dared to dream of a better life—a life where girls were valued and respected for their intelligence and strength.

In the end, Maya's journey served as a beacon of hope for girls everywhere, proving that with courage, determination, and a belief in oneself, anything is possible. And though her story may have started in a small village, its impact echoed across the world, inspiring generations of girls to reach for the stars and follow their dreams, no matter where they may lead.

CHAPTER NINETEEN

TODAY'S SCENARIO

Once upon a time, in the bustling city of Veridian, there existed a curious phenomenon known as the Whispering Walls. These ancient walls, adorned with intricate carvings and glyphs, held a mysterious power that allowed them to communicate with those who dared to listen.

Amelia, a young and adventurous historian, had always been fascinated by the tales surrounding the Whispering Walls. Determined to uncover their secrets, she embarked on a journey to Veridian, armed with only her knowledge and a thirst for discovery. Upon her arrival, Amelia was greeted by the sight of towering spires and winding streets, each corner hiding a piece of history waiting to be unearthed. Guided by rumors and ancient manuscripts, she soon found herself standing before the imposing facade of the Whispering Walls.

As she approached, a hush fell over the air, and the carvings on the walls seemed to shimmer with an otherworldly light. With bated breath, Amelia pressed her hand against the cold stone surface, closing her eyes as she focused on the whispers that danced in her mind.

The voices spoke of a forgotten kingdom, lost to time and buried beneath the city streets. They told of a powerful artifact, hidden within the depths of the earth, waiting for the one brave enough to claim it.

Driven by a newfound sense of purpose, Amelia delved deeper into the heart of Veridian, piecing together clues and unraveling the threads of ancient prophecy. Along the way, she encountered a colorful cast of characters – from eccentric scholars to streetwise urchins – each offering a piece of the puzzle that would lead her closer to her goal.

But the journey was not without its challenges. Dark forces lurked in the shadows, their eyes fixed on the same prize that Amelia sought. As she drew closer to the truth, she found herself ensnared in a web of intrigue and danger, forced to confront her fears and make impossible choices.

Yet through it all, Amelia remained undaunted, her spirit unbroken by the trials that lay before her. With unwavering determination, she pressed on, her heart set on uncovering the secrets of the Whispering Walls and unlocking the mysteries of Veridian's past.

And so, as the sun set on the horizon and the city lights began to twinkle like stars, Amelia stood at the threshold of destiny, ready to claim her place in history and discover the truth that lay hidden within the heart of Veridian.

WHISPERS OF TWILIGHT'S HAVEN"?

In fields of gold where dreams are sown,
And whispered secrets are gently blown,
The sun dips low, painting the sky,
With hues of orange, pink, and shy.
Amidst the tall grass, soft whispers play,
As the wind weaves tales at the end of the day.
The world slows down, time takes a rest,
In this tranquil haven, we are blessed.
The river's melody, a soothing refrain,
As it journeys forth, through valley and plain.
Reflecting the sky in its crystal embrace,

A mirror of heaven's eternal grace.
Birds in flight, a symphony high,
Their songs of freedom fill the sky.
In graceful arcs, they paint the air,
With wings of wonder, beyond compare.
As twilight deepens, stars appear,
Like diamonds strewn on velvet clear.
They twinkle softly, in cosmic delight,
Guiding lost souls through the night.
And in this realm, where dreams take flight,
Where day and night embrace the light,
We find solace in nature's embrace,
A sanctuary of peace and grace.

CHAPTER TWENTY-ONE

THE GREATEST SOUL

The greatest soul story is a tale as old as time, woven through the fabric of human existence. It begins with the birth of consciousness, a spark of divinity igniting within the depths of each soul. As the journey unfolds, souls traverse the realms of experience, navigating the labyrinth of emotions, relationships, and challenges. In the beginning, there was unity. Souls danced in the cosmic symphony, interconnected and harmonious. But as the cosmos expanded, the unity fragmented, and souls embarked on individual odysseys, seeking to rediscover their lost wholeness.

One such soul, named Aurora, descended into the earthly realm with a mission encoded in her essence – to spread love and light amidst the shadows of human existence. Born into a humble family, Aurora's radiance shone from an early age, touching the hearts of all who crossed her path.

Her journey was not without trials. In the tumult of adolescence, Aurora grappled with doubt and insecurity, questioning her purpose and place in the world. Yet, through the darkness, she discovered the power of resilience and inner strength, emerging from the shadows with newfound clarity and purpose.

As Aurora journeyed through life, she encountered kindred spirits and soul mates, each imparting wisdom and igniting the flame of remembrance within her heart. Together, they embarked on adventures across time and space, weaving a tapestry of experiences that transcended the limitations of mortal existence.

Yet, amidst the beauty and wonder, darkness lurked in the shadows, threatening to extinguish the light within. Aurora faced trials of the soul – betrayal, loss, and heartbreak – each a crucible forging her spirit into a beacon of compassion and understanding.

In the depths of despair, Aurora discovered the transformative power of forgiveness – both for others and herself. Through forgiveness, she reclaimed her power, transcending the limitations of her ego and embracing the boundless love that flowed through her being. Guided by intuition and the whispers of her soul, Aurora embarked on a pilgrimage of self-discovery, traversing the ancient landscapes of wisdom and enlightenment. Along the way, she encountered sages and mystics who imparted timeless truths, unlocking the secrets of the universe hidden within her own heart.

At the zenith of her journey, Aurora stood at the threshold of enlightenment, her spirit ablaze with the radiance of a thousand suns. In a moment of divine revelation, she realized that the greatest soul story was not one of individual triumph, but of collective awakening – a symphony of souls uniting in love and oneness.

With this realization, Aurora transcended the boundaries of time and space, merging her consciousness with the cosmic tapestry of existence. In her eternal dance with the cosmos, she became the embodiment of the greatest soul story – a timeless saga of love, light, and the eternal quest for truth.

CHAPTER TWENTY-TWO

THE ENIGMA OF THE CENTENNIAL CLOCK

In the heart of the quaint town of Millstone, there stood a majestic clock tower known as the Centennial Clock. It was a symbol of pride for the townsfolk, its intricate gears and golden hands marking time for over a century. However, on the eve of its hundredth anniversary, the clock stopped ticking, and its hands froze at midnight.

Detective Evelyn Stone, renowned for her keen intellect and sharp wit, was summoned to unravel the mystery. As she arrived in Millstone, she was greeted by Mayor Harrison, a man with a troubled expression etched upon his face.

"It's a disaster, Detective," the mayor lamented. "The Centennial Clock has stopped, and the town is in chaos. Everyone is counting on you to solve this puzzle before the grand centennial celebration tomorrow night."

With determination in her eyes, Evelyn accepted the challenge and set off to inspect the clock tower. As she examined the intricate machinery, she noticed something peculiar - a small, silver key lodged between the gears. It seemed out of place, as if intentionally placed to disrupt the clock's mechanism.

Her investigation led her to the town's historian, Professor Samuel Wright, who revealed a startling revelation. "Legend has it," he began, "that a century ago, on the night the Centennial Clock was unveiled, a thief attempted to steal its precious gears as a symbol of rebellion against the town's prosperity. But before he could succeed, he was apprehended and the gears were returned. However, the key to the clock's mechanism was never found." Evelyn's mind raced as she pieced together the clues. Could it be that the same thief or their descendant had returned to sabotage the clock once more?

With limited time remaining before the centennial celebration, Evelyn raced against the clock to uncover the truth. She interrogated suspects, analyzed fingerprints, and combed through old records in search of answers.

Finally, she discovered a hidden chamber beneath the clock tower, where she found the culprit - an elderly man with a striking resemblance to the thief from a century ago. With a confession in hand, Evelyn emerged triumphant, restoring the Centennial Clock to its former glory just in time for the grand celebration.

As the clock struck midnight, signaling the start of a new century, the townsfolk cheered, grateful to Detective Evelyn Stone for solving the enigma of the Centennial Clock and preserving their beloved landmark for generations to come.

WHISPERS OF THE HEART

In the stillness of the night,
Where moonbeams softly alight,
Whispers echo through the trees,
Carried on the gentle breeze.
Each leaf rustles its own tune,
Underneath the silver moon,
Secrets of the night unfold,
Stories that the stars have told.
In the silence, hearts converse,
In language plain, or in verse,
Emotions flow like rivers deep,
Where dreams and memories keep.
Echoes of a distant past,
Moments fleeting, yet they last,
Whispers of what's yet to be,
In the quiet, we are free.
Morning breaks, the spell is gone,
But in our hearts, it lingers on,
For in the whispers of the night,
We find solace, we find light.
So listen closely, you will hear,

The whispers that the heart holds dear,
A symphony of hopes and fears,
In whispers soft, the soul appears.

CHAPTER TWENTY-FOUR

A SONG OF SEASONS

In the spring's embrace, flowers bloom,
Awakening from winter's gloom,
Petals soft as morning dew,
Whispering secrets old and new.
Sun-kissed days and gentle rain,
Nurture growth on the verdant plain,
Life's symphony in full bloom,
Nature's canvas, no empty room.
Summer's heat and vibrant hues,
Paint the world in endless views,
Laughter echoes, hearts entwine,
Underneath the grapevine twine.
Autumn whispers, leaves descend,
Golden hues, a timeless blend,
The harvest moon in the twilight sky,
Whispers of a lullaby.
Winter's chill, a quiet hush,
Snowflakes fall in a graceful rush,
Silent nights and fireside cheer,
Whispers of the passing year.
Through seasons' dance, we find our way,
In whispers soft or bold display,
A song of life, a timeless rhyme,

In every season, every time.

JOURNEY OF THE SOUL

In the labyrinth of life we tread,
Where paths diverge and winds may lead,
A journey bound by time's embrace,
Through valleys deep and open space.
From tender dawn to twilight's hue,
Each step unveils a world anew,
Through joys that lift our spirits high,
And trials that teach us how to fly.
Seeking truths in shadows cast,
Moments cherished, memories amassed,
In laughter shared and tears unwept,
In promises kept and dreams unslept.
The heart, a compass, a steady guide,
Through oceans vast and mountains wide,
In solitude, we find our voice,
In echoes of a quiet choice.
For life is but a fleeting breath,
A tapestry of birth and death,
Yet in the tapestry, we weave,
Each thread a hope, each knot a leaf.
So let us walk with hearts aflame,

Embrace the wild, the tame, the same,
For in the journey, we are whole,
A symphony of heart and soul.

CHAPTER TWENTY-SIX

SHADOWS OF POWER

In the corridors where power reigns,
Where ambitions thrive and virtue wanes,
Politics dance a delicate dance,
Intrigue and deception, fate's cruel chance.
On marble floors, where echoes ring,
Whispers of alliances, secrets cling.
Masks adorned, identities veiled,
In the game of thrones, truth often derailed.
From podiums high, speeches resound,
Promises uttered, truths are drowned.
Rhetoric flows like a river wide,
Swirling currents where ideals collide.
Votes cast like stones in a turbulent sea,
Eager hands reaching for victory's key.
Campaigns waged with fervent might,
In the quest for justice, and what's right.
Yet shadows lurk in the corridors' gloom,
Where agendas hide in the crowded room.
Backroom deals and compromises made,
In the quest for power's elusive shade.
Citizens watch with hopeful eyes,

Yearning for change under partisan skies.
Democracy's heartbeat, a fragile beat,
Echoes in streets where convictions meet.
For politics, a stage both grand and bleak,
Where principles bend and courage speaks.
Amidst the turmoil, ideals ignite,
In the battle for justice, in the fight for rights.
So let the banners wave, let voices ring,
In the symphony of democracy's spring.
For in the heart of the political storm,
Hope flickers bright, for a new reform.

ECHOES OF DEMOCRACY

In the heart of the city, where buildings stand tall,
Lies the pulse of a nation, its rise and its fall.
Where streets are the veins, teeming with life,
And voices echo in the tumultuous strife.
In the halls of power, where decisions are made,
Lies the weight of the people, in ballots displayed.
Elections are the chorus, where hopes intertwine,
In the dance of democracy, a symphony is divine.
From town squares to debates, ideas collide,
In the arena of discourse, where passions reside.
Principles are the compass, guiding the way,
Through the fog of agendas, night turns to day.
Yet shadows loom large, where corruption creeps,
In the corridors of influence, where justice weeps.
Money whispers secrets, in the ears of the few,
While the many cry out, for what is true.
Leaders emerge, with promises bright,
To lead us forward, through the darkest night.
But power is a sword, with two-edged blades,
And trust can falter, in decisions made.
So let us cherish this fragile flame,
Of democracy's promise, in freedom's name.
Where every voice matters, in the grand design,
And liberty's echo is forever entwined.
For in the heartbeat of nations, through trials untold,
Lies the spirit of courage, resilience, and bold.
In the tapestry of history, woven with care,
We find the strength to rise, and the will to dare.

CHAPTER TWENTY-EIGHT

THE PENDULUM OF POWER

Part 1: The Election

In the heart of a bustling metropolis, where skyscrapers pierced the sky and neon lights bathed the streets in an ethereal glow, political ambitions simmered like the city's perpetual rush. It was an election year, and the atmosphere crackled with anticipation and fervor.

At the center of this political maelstrom stood Senator Alex Morgan, a charismatic figure whose silver tongue and steely resolve had propelled him from humble beginnings to the pinnacle of power. With a background in law and a knack for rallying public sentiment, Morgan had garnered a loyal following among both the elite and the working class.

Opposing him was Claire Thompson, a former corporate executive turned reformist politician. With a platform focused on social justice and economic equality, Thompson's rise had been swift, fueled by a wave of discontent among the city's marginalized communities and disillusioned youth.

As election day loomed closer, tensions mounted, and the city became a battleground of ideologies. Campaign rallies echoed through the streets, each candidate promising a brighter future while subtly casting shadows on their opponent's past.

Part 2: The Campaign Trail

Against this backdrop, Emily, a seasoned journalist with a penchant for uncovering truths buried beneath layers of rhetoric, found herself immersed in the whirlwind of the election. Assigned to cover Senator Morgan's campaign, she delved into the intricacies of his policies and the alliances that sustained his political machine.

Her investigations unearthed a web of backroom deals and whispered promises, where power brokers held sway over legislation and personal ambitions often eclipsed public welfare. Yet, amidst the smoke and mirrors, Emily glimpsed the genuine passion of Morgan's supporters, who saw in him a champion of stability and economic growth.

On the opposite side of the spectrum, Claire Thompson's campaign resonated with a younger demographic eager for change. Emily attended rallies where impassioned speeches rallied crowds to demand accountability from the establishment and envision a city where opportunities were not monopolized by the privileged few.

As the election drew nearer, Emily found herself torn between her role as a detached observer and her growing empathy for the stories of those whose lives would be shaped by the outcome. She wrote with a clarity that transcended partisan lines, capturing the hopes and fears of a city at a crossroads.

Part 3: The Debate

The crescendo of the election season arrived with a highly anticipated debate televised across the nation. In a dimly lit studio adorned with the flags of democracy, Senator Morgan and Claire Thompson faced off in a battle of words and ideologies that would sway undecided voters and solidify party allegiances.

Moderated by a seasoned journalist known for his incisive questions, the debate unfolded with a mixture of scripted rhetoric and unscripted revelations. Emily watched from the press gallery, scribbling notes furiously as the candidates sparred over healthcare reform, tax policy, and the widening wealth gap.

At one pivotal moment, Claire Thompson challenged Senator Morgan on his ties to corporate donors, citing campaign finance records that painted a picture of influence peddling behind closed doors. In response, Morgan deftly redirected the conversation to highlight Thompson's lack of experience in navigating the complexities of legislative negotiations.

The debate ended with no clear winner, leaving pundits and voters alike to dissect the nuances of each candidate's performance. For Emily, it marked a turning point in her coverage, as she delved deeper into the ramifications of political rhetoric and the fine line between conviction and compromise.

Part 4: Election Day

On the crisp morning of election day, Emily navigated through a sea of voters queued outside polling stations, their expressions a mosaic of determination and apprehension. She spoke with citizens from all walks of life, capturing their hopes for change or their desire to maintain the status quo.

As the day wore on, exit polls painted a picture of a city deeply divided. Lines blurred between party affiliations as individuals made their choices based on personal values, economic concerns, or simply a gut feeling about the candidates' sincerity.

By nightfall, the results began to trickle in. Emily watched alongside her fellow journalists as precinct after precinct reported their tallies. Senator Morgan maintained a slight lead in early counts, buoyed by strong support from suburban districts and established business interests.

But as votes from urban centers and youth-dominated precincts were tallied, Claire Thompson narrowed the gap, her message of change resonating with voters disillusioned by decades of political stagnation. It became increasingly clear that the outcome would hinge on turnout in key battlegrounds where every ballot counted.

Part 5: The Aftermath

In the early hours of the morning, with the city's skyline bathed in the first light of dawn, the final results were announced. Claire Thompson emerged victorious by a slim margin, becoming the city's first female mayor-elect. Her supporters erupted in jubilation, celebrating a triumph they saw as a mandate for progressive reform.

Senator Morgan conceded gracefully, pledging to work with the new administration for the betterment of the city he had served for so many years. In his concession speech, he spoke of unity and resilience, urging his supporters to embrace the democratic process and continue fighting for their beliefs.

For Emily, it was a moment of reflection amidst the whirlwind of deadlines and breaking news. She penned a poignant article capturing the essence of the election—a testament to the power of democracy and the enduring spirit of a city that dared to dream of a better future.

As the days turned into weeks and the city adjusted to its new leadership, Emily continued to report on the evolving political landscape. The pendulum of power had swung once more, setting the stage for new challenges and opportunities in a city where politics were not just a game, but a reflection of the hopes and aspirations of its people.

In Conclusion "The Pendulum of Power" is a tale of ambition, ideals, and the complexities of modern politics. It explores the dynamics of electoral campaigns, the clash of ideologies, and the transformative impact of democratic processes on individuals and communities. Through the lens of Emily's journalistic journey, the story delves into the human side of politics, where personal convictions and public service converge in the pursuit of a better tomorrow.

CHAPTER TWENTY-NINE

THE TRANQUIL POND: FINDING INNER PEACE

In the heart of a tranquil village nestled among emerald hills, there lived an elderly monk named Master Li. Master Li was known far and wide for his wisdom and serenity, and people would often seek his counsel on matters of the heart and spirit.

One crisp morning, a weary traveler named Mei arrived at the monastery where Master Li resided. Mei had been wandering the world in search of inner peace, but her heart felt heavy with doubts and uncertainties. She hoped that Master Li could offer her guidance on her journey.

Master Li welcomed Mei with a warm smile and invited her to sit by a tranquil pond shaded by ancient willow trees. The air was scented with the fragrance of blooming lotus flowers, and the gentle rustling of leaves provided a soothing backdrop to their conversation.

Mei poured out her heart to Master Li, sharing her struggles with finding purpose and meaning in life. She spoke of her fear of failure and her longing for a sense of fulfillment that seemed elusive.

Master Li listened intently, his eyes twinkling with understanding. He reached into the folds of his robe and withdrew a small, smooth stone. Holding it out to Mei, he said, "This stone represents your mind – clear, pure, and capable of reflecting the beauty of the world around you. Yet, like the surface of this pond, it can also be disturbed by ripples of doubt and worry."

Mei observed the stone in her palm, feeling its coolness against her skin. She nodded thoughtfully, sensing the deeper meaning behind Master Li's words.

"Close your eyes, Mei," Master Li continued, "and imagine yourself standing on the shore of this pond. Feel the warmth of the sun on your face and the gentle breeze caressing your skin. Now, with each breath you take, allow your mind to settle like the sediment in still water."

Mei followed Master Li's guidance, breathing deeply and focusing on the sensation of calm washing over her. Slowly, the worries that had weighed heavy on her heart began to dissipate like morning mist.

"Now," Master Li whispered softly, "imagine dropping that stone into the pond. Watch as it sinks deeper and deeper, disappearing into the depths where all is still and quiet. As it settles, notice how the surface of the pond becomes clear and reflects the world around it with perfect clarity."

Mei did as Master Li instructed, visualizing the stone sinking into the tranquil depths of the pond. With each passing moment, she felt a profound sense of peace enveloping her soul – a peace that transcended her fears and insecurities.

When Mei opened her eyes, she found herself gazing into Master Li's gentle gaze. Tears welled up in her eyes as she whispered, "Thank you, Master Li. I understand now that true peace comes from within, from letting go of the turbulence in my mind and embracing the serenity that lies beneath."

Master Li nodded knowingly, his smile radiant as the morning sun. "Remember, Mei," he said, "just as the pond reflects the beauty of the sky above, so too can your mind reflect the infinite possibilities that await you. Trust in the stillness within, and you will find the strength to navigate any storm."

With a heart brimming with newfound hope and clarity, Mei bid farewell to Master Li and resumed her journey. As she walked away from the monastery, she carried with her not just the wisdom imparted by Master Li, but also a deep-seated belief in her own inner strength and resilience.

And so, wherever life's journey took her, Mei knew that she carried within her the peaceful pond – a sanctuary of calm amidst the ebb and flow of life's challenges, a reminder that true peace begins and ends with the quiet courage to embrace the present moment.

THE FORGOTTEN WATCHMAKER

In the heart of a quaint village nestled between rolling hills and whispering forests, there lived a man named Theodore. He was known to all as the village watchmaker, a gentle soul with hands that moved with precision and eyes that held the wisdom of years spent with delicate mechanisms. Theodore's shop, tucked away on a cobblestone lane, was a haven of ticking clocks and chiming timepieces, where each piece told a story of its own.

From the earliest hours of dawn to the fading light of dusk, Theodore diligently worked on repairing and restoring clocks of all shapes and sizes. His shop was a treasure trove of nostalgia, adorned with antique pendulums swinging in rhythmic harmony and shelves lined with intricately crafted pocket watches adorned with ornate engravings. To Theodore, each tick and tock was a symphony, a testament to the passage of time and the beauty of craftsmanship.

Yet, behind his quiet demeanor and weathered hands, Theodore carried a secret—a longing that stirred within him like the gears of an old grandfather clock. For as long as he could remember, he had harbored dreams of creating a masterpiece—a timepiece that would transcend the boundaries of ordinary craftsmanship and capture the essence of time itself.

One fateful evening, as twilight painted the sky in hues of amethyst and gold, a stranger arrived at Theodore's shop. She was a young woman named Lila, her eyes alight with curiosity as she peered through the shop window at the intricate displays within. Lila had stumbled upon the village by chance, seeking refuge from a world filled with deadlines and expectations.

Intrigued by the stories whispered among the villagers of Theodore's skillful hands and the magic that flowed through his workshop, Lila ventured inside. She found Theodore hunched over an antique mantel clock, his spectacles perched precariously on the bridge of his nose as he delicately adjusted the minute hand. The warmth of the hearth cast dancing shadows across the room, enveloping them in a cocoon of tranquility.

Over time, Lila became Theodore's apprentice, her nimble fingers learning the delicate art of watchmaking under his patient guidance. As they worked side by side amidst the comforting tick-tock of timepieces, Theodore shared tales of his youth spent wandering through bustling markets and distant lands, where he had encountered master craftsmen and visionary artisans who had shaped his understanding of time and its infinite possibilities.

In return, Lila spoke of her own journey—a nomadic existence shaped by her wanderlust and insatiable thirst for knowledge. She recounted the thrill of discovering hidden bookshops tucked away in forgotten corners of ancient cities, where each dusty volume held secrets waiting to be unlocked. And she shared her dreams of capturing fleeting moments through the lens of her camera, freezing fragments of time in frames that spoke volumes of emotion and untold stories.

As seasons passed and the rhythm of their days melded into a symphony of shared dreams and quiet companionship, Theodore and Lila embarked on a journey to create their masterpiece—a timepiece that would transcend the boundaries of craftsmanship and weave together the threads of their shared experiences. Together, they explored forgotten techniques and experimented with unconventional materials, their minds ablaze with creativity and possibility.

On a crisp autumn morning, as the village lay blanketed in the first frost of the season, Theodore and Lila unveiled their creation—a grand clockwork marvel unlike anything the world had seen before. Its face was adorned with celestial motifs, each constellation meticulously etched into the delicate ivory dial. Its hands moved with a grace that mirrored the dance of planets, marking the passage of time with a whisper of serenity.

Word of their masterpiece spread like wildfire, drawing visitors from far and wide to Theodore's humble shop. Scholars marveled at the ingenuity of its design, while collectors vied for the opportunity to add it to their private collections. Yet, amidst the accolades and admiration, Theodore and Lila remained rooted in the simple joy of creation—the shared moments of inspiration and revelation that had forged an unbreakable bond between them.

As twilight descended upon the village once more, Theodore and Lila stood beneath the canopy of stars, their masterpiece shimmering in the moonlight. They knew that their journey had only just begun—that countless stories were waiting to be told, each one a testament to the enduring power of craftsmanship and the timeless allure of dreams.

And as they watched the village fade into silhouette against the canvas of the night sky, Theodore and Lila knew with certainty that they had found their place in the tapestry of time—a place where every tick and tock resonated with the echoes of their shared journey, and where the true essence of life lay not in the destination, but in the moments that shaped the journey itself.

CHAPTER THIRTY-ONE

THE ADVOCATE

JUSTICE FOR FREEDOM

In the quiet corridors of justice, where shadows often dwell,

Stands a figure strong and steadfast, where rights and
truths compel.
Their voice, a clarion call for those whose voices are
faint,
They champion for the marginalized, with courage
that knows no restraint.
With pen and paper as their sword, they navigate the
law,
Seeking fairness and equality, in every case they
draw.
They listen to the stories, the struggles, and the pain,
And weave them into narratives that justice can
sustain.
In courtrooms filled with tension, they speak with
eloquence and grace,
Presenting evidence and reason, to make injustice
erase.
They fight against oppression, against prejudice and
fear,
Their determination unwavering, their resolve always
clear.
Beyond the walls of legal battles, their advocacy
extends,
To communities and causes, where hope and change
amends.
They educate and empower, they uplift and they
defend,
Guiding through the darkness, until justice finds its
end.
So here's to the advocate, whose heart beats for the
right,
Whose compassion fuels their mission, through the
day and into night.

For in their tireless efforts, in the battles fought and
won,
They embody the spirit of justice, until the journey's
done.

CHAPTER THIRTY-TWO

"CELESTIAL BRUSHSTROKES: PAINTING THE UNIVERSE"

In strokes of color, whispers bold,
Canvas breathes, a tale retold.
Brush dances on the virgin white,
Emotions swirling, pure and bright.
A palette rich with dreams unseen,
Captures life, in shades between.
Sunset hues and midnight's gleam,
Each stroke a sigh, each hue a dream.
From depths of soul, the artist's gaze,
Creates a world, in a silent maze.
A portrait hangs in silent grace,
Eternal beauty, time can't erase.
In galleries where whispers flow,
Stories told, yet never know,
The artist's heart, the hidden part,
Bared in strokes, a work of art.

So cherish these, these painted lies,
For truth in art, in beauty lies.
A masterpiece, beyond compare,
In every stroke, a soul laid bare.

CHAPTER THIRTY-THREE

SPIRIT OF THE SWACHH BHARAT ABHIYAN

In the heart of India, where dreams ignite,
Lies a vision for all, pure and bright.
Clean streets and alleys, free from debris,
Where every soul thrives, healthy and free.
From north to south, east to west,
Every citizen joins, at their best.
A pledge to clean, a promise to keep,
Our country's beauty, forever deep.
Gandhi's dream, now our own,
To build a land where seeds are sown,
Not just of crops, but of respect,
For the earth and all that it begets.
Bins and brooms, in every hand,
Sweeping away filth from the land.
Not just a duty, but a call to unite,
To restore our nation's natural might.
Children learn, elders teach,
The value of a clean beach.

Mountains high and rivers pure,
Nature's gifts, we must secure.
Swachh Bharat, a journey long,
Yet together, we stand strong.
For a cleaner, greener, healthier land,
Hand in hand, we take our stand.

ETERNAL SHRINE: RAM MANDIR

In the heart of sacred Ayodhya's land,
Where stories of faith and destiny stand,
Rises a temple, centuries in waiting,
Amidst echoes of history, anticipating.
Ram Mandir, a shrine of ancient lore,
Where devotion flows forevermore,
From the banks of Sarayu's gentle flow,
To the heavens where divine winds blow.
In the temple's embrace, echoes resound,
Of Ram's courage, in battles unbound,

His love for Sita, a tale so true,
In each stone and pillar, eternally imbued.
Gleaming in the sunlight's golden hue,
Ram Mandir stands, majestic and true,
A symbol of unity, beyond earthly strife,
Where peace and harmony breathe new life.
As pilgrims gather, hearts filled with grace,
Their prayers ascend, finding their place,
In the sanctum where ideals unite,
Ram Mandir shines, a beacon of light.
In Ayodhya's embrace, timeless and grand,
Ram Mandir stands, a symbol so grand,
Of faith and culture, forever intertwined,
In every prayer, in every mind.
Thus, in the echoes of Ayodhya's call,
Ram Mandir rises, majestic and tall,
A testament to beliefs that endure,
In every heart, forever pure.

CHAPTER THIRTY-FIVE

WAVE OF WISDOM AND LIBERTY

In a land nestled between rolling hills and the endless expanse of the sea, where the sun painted the sky in hues of gold and crimson each evening, there dwelled a people whose spirits were shackled by the heavy chains of ignorance and oppression. For generations, they had labored under the rule of a tyrant whose decrees stifled their voices and cast shadows over their dreams.

Life in this land was a delicate balance of survival and silent suffering. The people whispered tales of a time when freedom danced on the wind like the leaves of the ancient oaks, but such memories had faded into myth as the tyrant's grip tightened. Yet, unbeknownst to them, a change was stirring in the depths of the ocean. Far beyond the horizon where the sea met the sky, a wave of extraordinary proportions began to take form. This wave was not born of ordinary currents; it shimmered with an otherworldly glow, as if infused with the very essence of wisdom and liberty itself.

As it surged towards the shore, its approach was heralded by a symphony of crashing waves and the song of seagulls soaring overhead. The people, drawn by an inexplicable sense of anticipation, gathered along the cliffs and beaches, their eyes fixed on the horizon where the wave loomed ever closer. When it finally reached the coast, its crest rose high into the sky, catching the rays of the setting sun and casting a dazzling display of colors across the water. At that moment, a hush fell over the assembled crowd as they witnessed something beyond their comprehension—a figure, radiant and majestic, standing amidst the spray of the wave.

It was the Spirit of Wisdom and Liberty, manifested in physical form to deliver a message of hope and empowerment to the beleaguered people. Clad in robes woven from the threads of the ocean's depths and the sky's expanse, the Spirit spoke not with words but with a profound presence that resonated deep within the souls of all who beheld it.

"Children of this land," the Spirit's voice echoed across the gathering, carried by the wind and waves, "I come bearing the gifts of wisdom and liberty, bestowed upon you by the forces of nature itself. Though you have known darkness, I bring you light. Though you have known chains, I bring you the key to unlock your potential."

The people listened with hearts heavy yet hopeful, their eyes reflecting the flickering flames of courage ignited by the Spirit's words. For the first time in years, they dared to believe that change was not only possible but imminent. With each passing day, the wave of wisdom and liberty continued to influence the land in profound ways. It swept away the cobwebs of ignorance and fear, replacing them with the seeds of knowledge and courage. Schools and academies sprang up like wildflowers in spring, nurturing the minds of the young and old alike with the teachings of history, science, and art.

The tyrant, sensing the shifting tides of fate, sought to quell the rising tide of dissent. But this time, the people were not cowed by threats or silenced by oppression. United by a newfound sense of purpose and guided by the Spirit's teachings, they stood firm against injustice, their voices blending into a chorus of defiance that echoed across the valleys and mountains. In the face of such unity and determination, the tyrant's power began to wane. His decrees lost their potency, and his forces found themselves outnumbered not by swords and shields, but by the sheer force of collective will and belief in a better future.

And so, the land that once languished in darkness and despair became a beacon of hope and enlightenment. The Spirit of Wisdom and Liberty, having fulfilled its mission to awaken the people's potential, retreated once more into the depths of the ocean, leaving behind a legacy carved in the annals of history.

Generations passed, but the memory of the wave of wisdom and liberty endured. It became a cornerstone of the land's identity—a testament to the resilience of its people and the transformative power of knowledge and freedom. Visitors from distant lands would hear tales of the miraculous wave that changed everything, and they would marvel at the spirit of a people who refused to surrender their dreams. And as the sun continued to set over the shores of this remarkable land, painting the sky in hues of gold and crimson, the echo of the Spirit's words lingered in the hearts of all who called it home: "Embrace knowledge, seek truth, and cherish freedom, for these are the pillars upon which your future shall be built."

CHAPTER THIRTY-SIX

PATHWAYS TO PROGRESS

"Pathways to Progress" was an initiative aimed at creating opportunities for underrepresented communities in urban centers. It started with a bold vision: to empower young adults from diverse backgrounds by providing them with the skills and resources needed to succeed in today's economy.

The program began in a bustling city neighborhood, where aspirations often clashed with limited opportunities. Sarah , a passionate community organizer, believed in the potential of every young person she encountered. She saw firsthand how a lack of access to education and job opportunities stifled ambition.

One summer morning, a group of teenagers gathered at the local community center for the launch of Pathways to Progress. They came from different walks of life—some from struggling families, others navigating the complexities of being first-generation immigrants. Among them was Jamal, a bright-eyed young man with dreams of becoming a software developer, despite his family's financial struggles.

The program offered resume-building workshops, interview skills, and financial literacy. Mentors from local businesses volunteered their time, sharing insights and opening doors to internships. Sarah tirelessly coordinated these efforts, ensuring each participant felt supported and inspired.

Over the weeks, Jamal and his peers soaked up knowledge like sponges. They learned not just about job skills, but also about resilience and determination. Challenges arose—transportation issues, doubts about their own abilities—but they persisted, buoyed by newfound confidence and a sense of community.

As summer turned to fall, success stories emerged. Jamal landed an internship at a tech startup, where his knack for coding impressed his mentors. Others secured jobs at local businesses, their futures transformed by Pathways to Progress's opportunities.

The initiative didn't just change individual lives; it revitalized the entire community. Businesses thrived with new, motivated employees. Families celebrated their children's achievements, inspired by the ripple effects of newfound hope.

Years later, Sarah reflected on the program's impact. The once skeptical neighborhood now buzzed with optimism. Jamal had become a role model for younger children, proof that with determination and support, dreams could indeed become reality. Pathways to Progress has shown that investing in youth meant investing in the future of the community. It proved that by opening doors and providing guidance, even the most marginalized could thrive. And as the sun set over the city skyline, it illuminated a pathway where progress and possibility intersected, creating a brighter tomorrow for all.

CHAPTER THIRTY-SEVEN

FUTURES REIMAGINED

In the quiet folds of time's embrace,
Where dreams and destinies interlace,
I glimpse a world where hope takes flight,
And shadows yield to the morning light.
Paths diverge, futures intertwine,
In the tapestry of fate's design,
Where every choice, each step we take,
Shapes the dawn and the day we make.
Through the veil of uncertainty,
We chart our course, yet still we see
The shimmering threads of what could be,
A tapestry is woven with possibility.
In this realm where dreams ignite,
And stars align with whispered might,
We carve our stories, bold and true,
In the boundless sky of azure blue.
For in our hearts, the future gleams,
A mosaic of hopes, a realm of dreams,
Where courage blooms and fears are stilled,
And every dreamer's heart is filled.
So let us dream and dare to soar,

To futures bright, forevermore,
For in the tapestry of our days,
Our dreams illuminate the way.
Let hope be our guiding star,
In futures reimagined, near and far,
For in each heartbeat, in each breath,
We find the courage to defy death.
In futures reimagined, we find our place,
Where love and laughter freely grace,
The paths we walk, the dreams we chase,
In futures reimagined, full of grace.

CHAPTER THIRTY-EIGHT

TECH, TRUTH, AND TRIBE

Once upon a time, in a world not so different from ours, there existed a vast kingdom where knowledge and technology reigned supreme. In this kingdom, the people were divided into tribes, each with their own beliefs about the nature of truth and the role of technology in their lives.

The first tribe, known as the Technocrats, believed fervently in the power of technology to solve all problems. They worshipped the latest gadgets and algorithms, seeing them as the keys to unlocking a utopian future. Led by their wise elders who were once engineers and scientists, they built towering cities of glass and steel, where artificial intelligence whispered in every corner and robotic servants catered to their every need.

On the other side of the kingdom, there lived the Ancestors. They were the keepers of ancient wisdom, passed down through generations in the form of stories and traditions. They believed in the importance of human connection and the wisdom of the natural world. They lived in harmony with the land, practicing ancient arts of healing and agriculture that had sustained their people for centuries.

Conflict brewed between these two tribes, fueled by their differing beliefs. The Technocrats scoffed at the Ancestors' reliance on old-fashioned ways, dismissing their practices as outdated and inefficient. They sought to bring the entire kingdom under the dominion of technology, believing it would lead to unparalleled progress and prosperity for all.

The Ancestors, in turn, feared that the rapid advance of technology would disrupt the delicate balance of nature and diminish the human spirit. They warned of a future where people became slaves to their creations, losing touch with what truly mattered in life. Amidst this growing tension, there arose a young scholar named Elena. She belonged to neither tribe, yet she felt a deep curiosity about both their perspectives. Elena spent her days studying the ancient texts of the Ancestors and the cutting-edge theories of the Technocrats. She wondered if there could be a way to bridge the gap between these two worlds.

One fateful day, a great storm swept through the kingdom, threatening to destroy everything in its path. The Technocrats scrambled to deploy their technological defenses, while the Ancestors turned to their ancient rituals to appease the wrath of the elements. But neither approach seemed enough to halt the fury of nature.

In the midst of the chaos, Elena had an epiphany. She realized that both tribes held valuable truths — the Technocrats in their mastery of science and innovation, and the Ancestors in their deep connection to the rhythms of the natural world. She brought leaders from both tribes together, urging them to combine their strengths and knowledge.

Through collaboration and mutual respect, they devised a plan that blended advanced technology with ancient wisdom. The Technocrats developed sophisticated weather prediction systems, while the Ancestors provided insights into the subtle signs of nature's balance. Together, they were able to mitigate the storm's destructive force and protect their kingdom.

From that day on, the tribes learned to coexist peacefully, recognizing that truth and progress could emerge from the intersection of their different perspectives. Elena became known as the bridge-builder, and her story was passed down through generations as a reminder of the power of unity in diversity. And so, in the kingdom where knowledge and technology reigned supreme, the story of tech truth and tribes became a testament to the importance of embracing multiple truths and finding harmony amidst diversity.

CHAPTER THIRTY-NINE

MOONLIT SERENADE

Beneath the velvet cloak of night,
Where stars ignite their silent light,
A silver orb hangs soft and high,
Casting shadows, painting sky.
The moon, a mistress to the sea,
In whispered tones calls out to me,
A serenade of tranquil grace,
In every shimmer, every trace.
Her gentle touch on land and sea,
A timeless dance, a melody,
Of dreams that weave through midnight's air,
Soft whispers carried everywhere.
In quiet corners, secrets keep,
Where lovers sigh and poets weep,
The moon, a guide through darkest hours,
Unveiling paths, revealing powers.
And as she wanes or waxes bright,
In waxing crescent or full delight,
Her luminescence, pure and clear,
Dispels the doubts, always the fear.
So let us bask in moonlit glow,
On tranquil nights where dreams may flow,
And hear the moon's sweet serenade,

In silence found, in love conveyed.

ETERNAL DANCE

In the heart of the forest's embrace,
Where sunlight filters through leaves' lace,
A dance unfolds in dappled light,
Between the shadows, day and night.
The trees, sway in a gentle breeze,
Whispering secrets among the leaves,
Roots entwined in ancient ground,
A symphony of life profound.
Creatures small and creatures grand,
In harmony, they make their stand,
From fleeting butterfly to mighty bear,
Each finds its place, each has its share.
And in this tapestry so grand,
Life's interconnected strands,
A timeless rhythm, a cosmic flow,
Where beginnings and ends softly glow.
So listen closely to the song,
That nature sings, both loud and long,
For in the forest's quiet trance,
SWe find ourselves in the eternal dance.

CHAPTER FORTY-ONE

THE STARLIT PATH

A young boy named Landon lived in a village nestled between rolling hills and whispering meadows. He had a curious spirit and a heart filled with dreams that danced like fireflies in the night sky. But among all his dreams, one shimmered brighter than the rest: to walk the legendary Starlit Path.

The Starlit Path was said to appear once every century, a trail of glowing stardust that led to a hidden realm where wishes came true. It was a path sought by adventurers and dreamers alike, but none had returned to tell their tales.

Undeterred by the warnings of elders, Landon set off one moonlit night, following the whispers of the wind and the gentle guidance of the stars. His journey took him through dense forests where ancient trees whispered ancient secrets, across shimmering rivers where water nymphs sang lullabies, and over misty mountains where dragons slumbered.

Along the way, Landon encountered companions both strange and wondrous. There was Ember, a mischievous sprite who danced on sunbeams and knew every secret of the forest; Olin, a wise old owl who shared tales of the stars and their constellations; and Lyra, a kind-hearted healer who tended to wounded creatures with gentle hands and soothing words.

Together, they faced trials and tribulations: riddles posed by cunning sphinxes, storms conjured by vengeful spirits, and illusions spun by trickster faeries. Through each challenge, Landon's resolve grew stronger, fueled by the hope that the Starlit Path would lead him to his deepest desire.

As they approached the final stretch of their journey, the path shimmered before them like a bridge of dreams woven from moonbeams. Each step resonated with the echoes of forgotten wishes and untold stories, beckoning them closer to the realm beyond.

At last, they reached the end of the Starlit Path—a vast, ethereal garden bathed in the soft glow of a thousand stars. Here, whispers of wishes floated on the breeze, carrying with them the hopes and dreams of all who had walked before.

In the center of the garden stood a solitary figure—a Weaver of Dreams—who spun threads of stardust into shimmering tapestries that adorned the sky. With a knowing smile, the Weaver greeted Landon and his companions, their presence a testament to the power of dreams and the strength of friendship.

Landon approached the Weaver, his heart brimming with gratitude and wonder. With a voice as clear as crystal and as gentle as a breeze, he spoke his wish into the quiet night. And as the stars twinkled in approval, the Weaver nodded, weaving Landon's wish into the fabric of the universe.

As dawn painted the sky in hues of pink and gold, Landon and his companions bid farewell to the Starlit Path. Though their journey had come to an end, their hearts were forever changed by the magic they had witnessed and the bonds they had forged.

Back in the village, Landon shared his tale with wide-eyed children and skeptical elders alike. Some dismissed it as a mere fantasy, while others listened with a spark of hope in their eyes. But Landon knew the truth—the Starlit Path existed not only in distant realms but also within the hearts of those who dared to dream.

As the years passed, Landon became a guardian of dreams, guiding others on their journeys of discovery and wonder. For he knew that beneath the veil of reality, the world shimmered with untold possibilities, waiting for those brave enough to follow their dreams along the Starlit Path.

CHAPTER FORTY-TWO

"ECHOES OF SOCIETY"

In the labyrinth of city streets, we weave,
Where masks of polished smiles deceive,
Each soul a solitary star in a crowded night,
Seeking connection in the neon light.
Towers of glass reflect our aspirations high,
Yet shadows lurk where dreams and truth comply,
In boardrooms where power plays its game,
And whispers echo with ambition's name.
Faces pass, each a story untold,
Striving, surviving, in the relentless fold,
From bustling markets to quiet lanes,
A tapestry of joys, sorrows, and pains.
Where wealth and poverty interlace,
And echoes of history leave their trace,
Society, a complex, shifting sea,
Where currents of change shape destiny.
But beneath the veneer of status and gain,
Lie hearts that bleed, and souls in pain,
Yearning for kinship, for meaning true,
In this grand mosaic of me and you.
So let us build bridges, tear down walls,

Heed humanity's silent calls,
For in unity lies our strength and grace,
In this shared journey through time and space.

CHAPTER FORTY-THREE

BUILDERS OF TOMORROW: AN ODE TO ENGINEERING MINDS

TODAY'S CHILDREN TOMORROW'S FUTURE

In the workshop of the mind, where ideas ignite,

Lies in the engineer's domain, where logic takes
flight.
In circuits of thought, where innovation gleams,
Where dreams are forged from abstract schemes.
With the precision of mind and a steady hand,
They craft solutions where others see land.
From gears that whisper in mechanical song,
To bridges that span where rivers belong.
In algorithms intricate, they find the way,
To unravel mysteries, day by day.
They measure, they calculate, they refine,
Creating futures where possibilities align.
In the quiet of labs, where theories unfold,
They push the boundaries, fearless and bold.
For in the heart of each machine they design,
Lies the essence of their grand design.
So here's to the engineers, architects of tomorrow,
Who shapes our world, banishing sorrow.
With minds ablaze and hearts aglow,
They build the future, we've yet to know.

CHAPTER FORTY-FOUR

"SCHOOL DAYS: A JOURNEY THROUGH YOUTH'S CANVAS"

In halls where echoes of laughter ring,
And desks bear the weight of burgeoning dreams,
There lies a world of youthful wonder,
Where every day sparks a new adventure.
In classrooms adorned with knowledge's light,
Teachers ignite minds with wisdom bright.
Pages turn, revealing secrets untold,
As curiosity blossoms, young and bold.
Friendships forged in the fires of time,
Shared secrets whispered in rhythm and rhyme.
Playgrounds echo with joyful cries,
Underneath boundless, azure skies.
Lessons learned, both in books and in play,
Mistakes were made along the winding way.
Challenges met with courage unfurled,
In the dance of a swiftly turning world.
Memories carved in the annals of youth,
Treasures stored, tokens of simple truth.

School days fade as years swiftly pass,
Leaving imprints on hearts of glass.
Oh, school days, a tapestry spun,
Of growth, of learning, of battles won.
In the tapestry of life, forever enshrined,
The echoes of school days, are forever entwined.

CHAPTER FORTY-FIVE

"RIPPLES OF REFLECTION: A POEM ON WATER"

Beneath the heavens' azure sweep,
Where sunlight dances on the deep,
Lies a world both gentle and wild,
Where water flows, serene and mild.
From mountain peaks where glaciers gleam,
Rivers birthed in sunlit streams,
Carving canyons, valleys wide,
In their rush, no place to hide.
Lakes that mirror the sky's expanse,
Reflecting clouds in tranquil dance,
Their depths conceal a mystery,
Life's cradle in aqueous symphony.
Ocean vast, horizon's edge,
Where waves embrace with the rhythmic pledge,
A boundless realm of azure hue,
Awash with tales both old and new.
In raindrops' fall, a whispered call,
To nourish the earth, renewing all,

In rivers' flow, a constant hum,
Life's pulse is where the past and future come.
Water, the essence of our birth,
On this blue planet, spinning earth,
From droplets small to oceans wide,
In every form, our world's guide.

"SILENT REVERIE: THE BACKBENCHER'S REFLECTION"

In the shadowed realm where whispers weave,
Where backbenchers quietly deceive,
Unseen by eyes that seek the light,
They dwell in corners, out of sight.
Not at the forefront, nor leading the fray,
Yet in their silence, wisdom may lay.
Observing the dance of power and sway,
They ponder the world in their way.
Away from the spotlight's glaring gaze,
They navigate life's intricate maze.
Their thoughts, like rivers, flow deep and slow,
Unraveling mysteries others don't know.
Behind the scenes, they hold their ground,
In quiet rebellion, they are found.
Their voices were soft, yet not unheard,
Resonate deeply with every word.
For in the symphony of noise and cheer,
The backbencher's silence rings clear.
A pause, a breath, a moment of grace,
In their stillness, find their place.
So let us not dismiss or disregard,
The wisdom of those who stand apart.
For in the chorus of loud acclaim,
Backbenchers carve their names.

"EMBERS OF INDEPENDENCE"

In the heart's expanse, where courage springs,
Lies the quest for freedom, where the soul sings.

Independence, a beacon, fiercely ablaze,
Ignites the spirit through life's maze.
Not bound by chains of doubt or fear,
But by the dreams that draw us near.
To carve our path, bold and true,
In every step, the self renewed.
From the shackles of conformity,
We break free, embracing unity.
With each choice, a sovereign decree,
Crafting our fate, wild and free.
In solitude or the midst of the crowd,
Independence whispers strong and loud.
A celebration of strength untold,
In every heartbeat, a story unfolds.
So raise the banner, let it fly,
Independence is our battle cry.
For in our hearts, the flame will burn,
Forevermore, our spirits yearn.

CHAPTER FORTY-EIGHT

"SHADOWS OF VIOLENCE: A CRY FOR PEACE"

In the darkened alleys where shadows breed,
Lurks are a specter born of human need.
With clenched fists and hearts of stone,
Violence reaps what's never sown.
It prowls the streets with silent tread,
Leaving scars on souls, a trail of dread.
Its voice a shout, its touch a blow,
Leaving wounds that bleed and grow.
From whispered threats to screams of pain,
Echoes of turmoil, like pouring rain.
In shattered homes and broken hearts,

Violence tears lives apart.
Yet amidst the chaos, a flicker of light,
A plea for peace in the midst of the night.
For in each heart, a spark remains,
A hope that love can break these chains.
Let us rise against this tide of hate,
Before it seals humanity's fate.
With courage strong and voices clear,
Let's banish violence, far and near.
For in unity, we'll find the key,
To build a world where all are free.
Where kindness reigns and hearts unite,
And violence fades into the night.

CHAPTER FORTY-NINE

"DIGITAL REVERIE"

In the palm of our hands, a world unfolds,
Where wires weave dreams and tales untold.
A marvel of metal, circuits in flight,
Boundless in reach, from day to night.
Silent whispers through digital air,
Connections sparked with a touch, so rare.
A pocket-sized portal, a gateway to roam,
Infinite possibilities find a home.
In pixels and glass, reflections gleam,
Mirroring hopes, in this digital stream.
Maps that guide through cities unknown,
A compass true, in the world we've grown.
Voices echo across the divide,
Across oceans wide, with nothing to hide.
Messages dance with the speed of thought,
Where once was distant, now is brought.
Yet amidst the glow of screens, we stare,
Do we lose touch, do we truly care?
For in the embrace of the mobile's glow,
Do we find solace, or does it show?
A modern marvel, our lifeline, our guide,
In its presence, our worlds collide.
But remember amidst its shining facade,

To grasp the real, not just the mod.
For in the palm of our hands, as we delve,
Let's cherish connections that serve us well.
In this realm where the virtual and real align,
May our mobiles be bridges, not walls divine.

CHAPTER FIFTY

THE STILLNESS WITHIN

In the quiet chambers of the mind,
Where thoughts like gentle rivers unwind,
Lies a sanctuary of peace profound,
Where silence whispers, all around.
During the chaos, a tranquil retreat,
Where the heart finds solace, in rhythm's beat.
Breath becomes a bridge, to inner calm,
As the soul discovers its healing balm.
With each inhale, tension ebbs away,
In the exhale, worries gently sway.
Mindfulness blooms, like flowers in bloom,
In the garden of serenity, beyond the gloom.
Time stands still, in this sacred space,
Where worries vanish, without a trace.
As awareness deepens, clarity dawns,
In the quietude, where peace spawns.
Embrace the stillness, let thoughts dissolve,
In the silence, mysteries resolve.
Find refuge in the present moment's grace,
Where the essence of being finds its place.
Meditation, a journey inward, profound,

Where the soul's wisdom can be found.
In the sanctuary of the mind's retreat,
The stillness within was so pure, so sweet.

CHAPTER FIFTY-ONE

SCIENCE, SOCIETY, AND SOVEREIGNTY

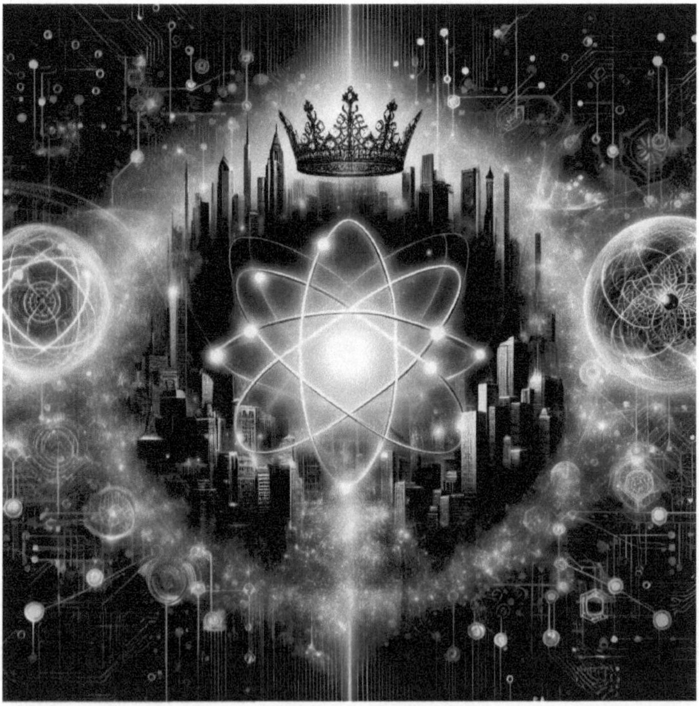

In labs where minds in silence dwell,
Where atoms dance and secrets swell,
Science unfurls its curious might,
To pierce the veils of the darkest night.
Yet in the streets where voices cry,
Society questions, and wonders why
The fruits of knowledge, are so profound,
Are weighed by morals tightly bound.
Sovereignty, with steady hand,
Guides the ship to charted land,
It sets the rules, it draws the line,
To harness truth, to redefine.
But can it yield to science bold,
Or bend to pressures, new and old?
For powers clash where realms collide,
Innovation at tradition's side.
Science, with its relentless quest,
Seeks truths that none have yet confessed,
While society, with heart and soul,
Nurtures truths that make us whole.
And sovereignty, in governance strong,
Must balance rights with progress long,
To shape a world where all may thrive,
Where science and society survive.
In this dance of hopes and fears,
Across the span of countless years,
Let wisdom guide each step we take,
For science, society, and sovereignty's sake.

CHAPTER FIFTY-TWO

THE FORGOTTEN KEY

In the heart of an ancient forest, where sunlight filtered through the canopy in shards of gold and green, there lay a secret buried deep within the roots of time itself—a secret guarded by whispers of the wind and the ancient trees. This secret was known only as the Forgotten Key.

Legends whispered of its existence, of a key that held the power to unlock not just doors, but entire realms of forgotten knowledge and untold wonders. Many had sought it, drawn by the promise of its transformative power, yet none had succeeded in unraveling the mystery that shrouded it.

Mara was not like the others in her village. While her peers played in the sunlit meadows, she would often wander into the dense woods, trailing her fingers along the rough bark of ancient trees, listening intently to the murmurs of unseen spirits. Her curiosity was insatiable, her thirst for knowledge unquenchable.

It was during one of these solitary explorations that Mara stumbled upon an old manuscript hidden within the hollow of a great oak tree. The manuscript, faded and fragile, spoke of the Forgotten Key in hushed tones, describing it as a catalyst for change, a bridge between the known and the unknown.

Determined to uncover the truth behind the legends, Mara sought the counsel of Old Arlen, the village sage whose eyes held the wisdom of ages past. Together, they deciphered cryptic clues scattered across ancient texts and maps, piecing a trail that led deep into the heart of the forest.

Their journey was fraught with peril—a labyrinth of twisting paths guarded by mythical beasts and treacherous terrain. Yet Mara pressed on, fueled by a sense of purpose that burned brighter with each step. Along the way, she forged alliances with unlikely companions—a mischievous sprite who danced on moonbeams and a stoic guardian spirit with eyes like smoldering embers.

As they delved deeper, Mara began to unravel not only the secrets of the Forgotten Key but also the mysteries of her lineage. She discovered that she was descended from a line of ancient guardians tasked with protecting the key from falling into the wrong hands. The weight of this revelation settled upon her shoulders like a mantle of stars.

In the heart of the forest, amidst the ruins of an ancient temple overgrown with moss and vines, Mara finally stood before the pedestal upon which the Forgotten Key rested. Its surface gleamed with an otherworldly radiance, shimmering with untapped potential and dormant magic.

But their journey had not gone unnoticed. Dark forces stirred in the shadows, drawn by the allure of the key's power. A shadowy figure emerged—a sorcerer cloaked in darkness, his eyes gleaming with a hunger that mirrored the abyss. He sought to claim the key for himself, to bend its power to his will and unleash chaos upon the world.

In a climactic battle that shook the very foundations of the forest, Mara and her companions fought valiantly against the sorcerer and his minions. Spells flashed like lightning, echoing through the ancient trees as the fate of the key hung in the balance. With each incantation, Mara felt the weight of her ancestors' legacy urging her onward, guiding her hand with ancient wisdom.

In the end, it was not brute force that prevailed but the strength of Mara's conviction and the bonds forged through friendship and trust. With a final surge of determination, Mara unleashed the true potential of the Forgotten Key—not to conquer, but to heal and restore balance to the world.

As the sorcerer retreated into the shadows, defeated but not vanquished, Mara made her decision. With solemn reverence, she entrusted the key to its rightful guardians—the spirits of the forest who had watched over it since time immemorial. And as dawn broke over the horizon, casting a golden glow upon the treetops, Mara knew that her journey had only just begun.

"The Forgotten Key" became more than a legend—it became a testament to the resilience of the human spirit and the power of knowledge to shape destinies. And as Mara returned to her village, the whispers of the wind carried her name across the land, a beacon of hope and courage for generations to come.

CHAPTER FIFTY-THREE

THE VISIONARY VELI

Chapter 1: A Gift Revealed

In the bustling town of Eldoria, nestled between rolling hills and whispering forests, lived a young artisan named Veli. Veli was known for crafting exquisite jewelry, each piece telling a story of creativity and resilience. Yet, there was more to Veli than met the eye. From a young age, Veli possessed a rare gift - the ability to see glimpses of the future.

These visions came unexpectedly, triggered by emotions or significant events. Sometimes they were clear and vivid, like watching scenes unfold before Veli's eyes; other times, they were fleeting and cryptic, leaving Veli puzzled and anxious. Despite this extraordinary ability, Veli kept it a closely guarded secret, fearing how others might react if they knew.

One crisp autumn morning, as Veli was collecting colorful leaves for a new jewelry design, a vision struck with unusual clarity. Veli saw the town square engulfed in flames, people screaming in panic, and buildings crumbling. The intensity of the vision shook Veli to the core. It wasn't the first time Veli had seen a disaster, but this one felt different - closer, more urgent.

Terrified yet determined, Veli hurried home and began sketching feverishly. Designs flowed from Veli's mind onto paper, each piece intricately detailed with symbols and patterns that mirrored the vision. These were not just ordinary designs; they were a warning, a plea for the town to prepare.

Chapter 2: A Town in Disbelief

As Veli worked tirelessly to create the jewelry, rumors spread through Eldoria of a coming disaster. Whispers of Veli's visions reached skeptical ears, met with dismissive laughs and raised eyebrows. The townspeople admired Veli's craftsmanship but doubted the validity of these prophetic warnings.

One evening, Veli gathered the courage to approach Mayor Aron, a respected figure known for his pragmatism and skepticism. With trembling hands, Veli presented the designs and recounted the vision with unwavering conviction. The mayor listened attentively, his brow furrowing in contemplation.

"This is quite... extraordinary, Veli," Mayor Aron finally spoke, his voice measured. "But visions? Prophecies? This town has prospered for generations without such fanciful tales."

Veli pleaded earnestly, recounting details from the vision that only Veli could know. Despite Veli's sincerity, doubt lingered in the mayor's eyes. He promised to consider the warning but made no commitment to act.

Distressed but undeterred, Veli turned to the townspeople. Some offered sympathetic nods, while others shook their heads in disbelief. The divide between those who believed and those who doubted grew wider, casting a shadow over Eldoria.

Chapter 3: The Calm Before the Storm

Days turned into weeks, and Eldoria resumed its tranquil rhythm. Veli continued to create jewelry, each piece infused with a silent plea for preparedness. The town square bustled with merchants and children playing, oblivious to the looming threat that Veli foresaw.

Yet, as Veli walked the cobblestone streets, unease gnawed at their heart. The visions had never been wrong before. What if this time was no different? What if Eldoria faced a catastrophe that could have been prevented?

One chilly evening, while Veli was gazing at the stars, a sudden vision seized Veli's senses. This time, it was not a disaster but a moment of profound clarity. Veli saw the townspeople coming together, united by a common purpose. They were building barriers, stockpiling supplies, and organizing evacuation routes. Hope blossomed amidst uncertainty, fueled by Veli's unwavering belief in the power of foresight.

With renewed determination, Veli decided to take matters into their own hands. Gathering a small group of believers, Veli began preparing for the worst, hoping beyond hope that their visions would prove unnecessary.

Chapter 4: The Day of Reckoning

The fateful day arrived with a chilling dawn. Dark clouds gathered on the horizon, and a sense of foreboding hung heavy in the air. Veli stood in the town square, heart pounding as the townspeople watched with a mixture of curiosity and skepticism.

Suddenly, a distant rumble echoed through the valley, followed by a deafening roar. A landslide, triggered by heavy rains, thundered down the mountainside towards Eldoria. Panic swept through the crowd as people scrambled for safety.

In that moment of chaos, Veli's preparations proved invaluable. Evacuation routes guided people to safety, barriers held back the rushing waters, and supplies provided comfort amidst uncertainty. The town, once divided by doubt, now stood united against nature's fury.

As the last echoes of disaster faded, Mayor Aron approached Veli with a mixture of awe and humility. "You saw this coming, didn't you?" he asked quietly, eyes searching for answers in Veli's gaze.

Veli nodded solemnly, feeling the weight of their gift more than ever. "I saw what could happen," Veli replied softly. "And I couldn't bear to let it unfold without trying to make a difference."

Chapter 5: A New Beginning

In the aftermath of the disaster, Eldoria emerged stronger and more resilient than before. The town honored Veli's foresight with gratitude and respect, recognizing the gift that had once been a source of skepticism.

Veli continued to create jewelry, each piece now imbued with hope and resilience. The designs no longer foretold disasters but celebrated unity and solidarity. Veli's workshop became a symbol of inspiration, drawing visitors from far and wide who marveled at the craftsmanship and the story behind each creation.

With time, the memory of the disaster faded, but Veli's legacy endured. The town of Eldoria learned to embrace differences and recognize the potential within each individual. Veli's gift, once a burden carried in solitude, became a beacon of light that guided Eldoria through challenges and triumphs.

And so, in the heart of Eldoria, Veli's story echoed through generations, a testament to the power of vision and the strength found in unity.

CHAPTER FIFTY-FOUR

SONGS OF SOLITUDE

In solitude's embrace, a symphony I hear,
Echoes of silence, whispers crystal clear.
Notes woven gently in the fabric of night,
Songs of solitude, a tranquil delight.
The rustle of leaves, a gentle refrain,
Softly serenading a heart's silent pain.
Melodies linger in the cool evening air,
A solitary dance with shadows, so rare.
Each chord resonates with a soul's soft plea,
A quiet crescendo of memories set free.
In the stillness, where dreams softly tread,
Echoes of solace, where hearts are fed.
Songs of solitude, a tranquil embrace,
Embers of solace in a sacred space.
A timeless melody, serene and pure,
In solitude's symphony, I find the cure.

CHAPTER FIFTY-FIVE

ENCHANTMENT COMPASS

In realms where moonlight softly weaves,
Enchantment blooms among the leaves.
Whispers dance on the evening breeze,
Where magic hums beneath the trees.
Stars above, like diamonds bright,
Paint the canvas of the night.
Spellbound hearts, in rapture's trance,
Find the world in a mystic dance.
Lanterns of forgotten lore,
Guide us to an ancient shore.
Where echoes of the past entwine,
With futures woven, and intertwined.
In realms where dreams and reality blend,
Enchantment's song will never end.
For in the heart where wonder gleams,
Lies the essence of enchanted dreams.

HARMONY'S ARCHITECT: ODE TO A COORDINATOR

In the heart of plans and schemes,
Where order reigns and vision gleams,
Stands a figure, steadfast and true,
Weaving threads of tasks anew.
Coordinator, with a steady hand,
Maps the course across the land.
Guiding teams with skill and grace,
In the dance of time and space.
From chaos blooms a structured art,
Crafted by your careful heart.
Binding goals with threads of light,
Turning the day from dark to bright.
Oh, coordinator, silent guide,

In your presence, worlds collide.
Effort shaped, and dreams take flight,
In the symphony of day and night.
Through the cycles, seasons turn,
Lessons learned, and wisdom earned.
In the tapestry that you weave,
Lies the truth that we believe.
Coordinator, soul profound,
In your orbit, all are bound.
In the quiet of your nameless grace,
Lives in the heart of every place.

INK AND PAPER

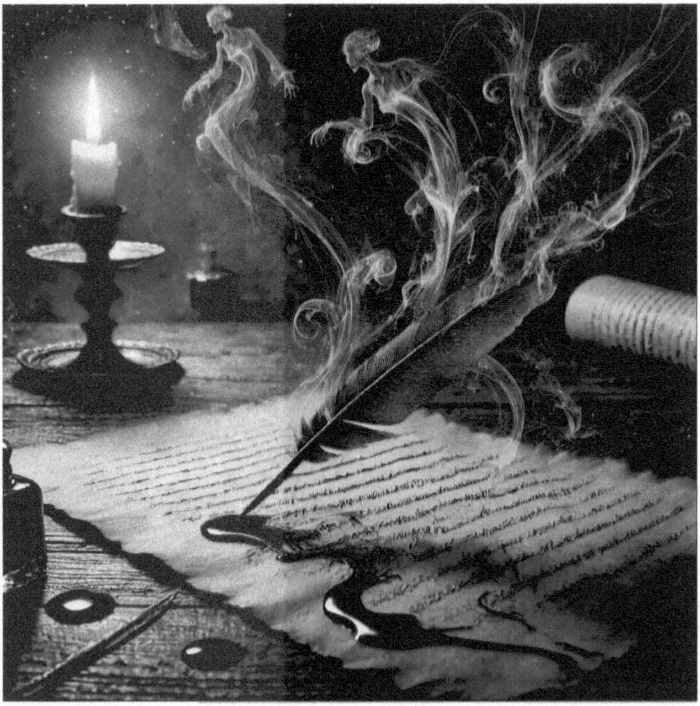

PEN'S IMAGINATION

In the quiet dawn, the press hums low,
A symphony of stories, in a row,
Ink spills like secrets on crisp, white sheets,
Whispers of the world in hurried beats.
Lines of black against a canvas pale,
Tales of triumph, of loss, of hope, and fail,
Each headline a beacon, each column a thread,
Connecting us all, the living and the dead.
With coffee in hand, we unfold the past,
Pages turning gently, moments held fast,
From distant lands to our own front door,
The heartbeat of life, the pulse of the lore.
But in this digital age, where whispers can fade,
The printed word fights, though some are afraid,
For still, there's a magic in paper's embrace,
In stories that linger, in time and in space.
So here's to the newspaper, old friend and guide,
A keeper of memories, where truth will reside,
May your ink never dry, your stories ignite,
For in every fold, there's a spark of the light.

ROOTS IN THE SAND

In the whisper of the waves, where the shoreline
bends,
A tale of resilience, where the ocean extends.
Beneath the sun's warm gaze, where the tides gently
play,
There lie the roots of dreams, in the sand, they sway.

They anchor deep in silence, where the grains softly
gleam,
Holding fast to the whispers of a long-forgotten dream.
With every crashing wave, they dance to nature's tune,
A symphony of hope beneath the watchful moon.
Though storms may rage and fury rise, they bend but
do not break,
For in the heart of struggle, new strength is born to
wake.
Each grain, a memory; each tide, a story spun,
Of those who found their purpose, in the warmth of the
sun.
When footprints fade with daylight and the evening
draws near,
The roots remain unyielding, in the sand, they
persevere.
For even in the shifting, in the currents that ensue,
There lies a steadfast promise that tomorrow brings
anew.
So let us plant our stories where the sea meets the
land,
Embrace the ties that bind us, like those roots in the
sand.
For life, like waves, is fleeting, but the heart's embrace is
grand,
And in the depths of our being, we are all forever
spanned.

CHAPTER FIFTY-NINE

THE ADVOCATE'S DAUGHTER

In the bustling city of Verenthia, where skyscrapers touched the clouds and dreams often collided with harsh realities, lived Maya, the daughter of a renowned human rights advocate, Elena Rodriguez. From a young age, Maya was surrounded by the fervent discussions of justice, equality, and the relentless pursuit of truth that filled their home.

A Life of Inspiration

Elena was a fierce advocate, known for her tireless work defending marginalized communities and fighting against systemic injustices. She often took Maya with her to rallies, courtrooms, and community meetings, instilling in her a strong sense of purpose. Maya admired her mother deeply but sometimes felt the weight of her legacy pressing down on her shoulders.

As Maya grew older, she grappled with the expectations that came with being the advocate's daughter. She was expected to follow in her mother's footsteps, to be outspoken and fearless. But Maya had a quiet spirit; she preferred to express herself through art, capturing emotions and stories on canvas. The pressure to choose between her passion and her mother's vision created an internal conflict that left her feeling torn.

A Defining Moment

One evening, after a particularly intense day of protests, Elena returned home, her eyes ablaze with passion. "Maya," she said, "there's a community meeting tomorrow about the housing crisis in our city. We need to stand up for those who can't."

Maya hesitated. "I want to support you, Mom, but I don't know if I can speak like you do. I express myself through my art."

Elena smiled gently. "Art is powerful, my dear. It can inspire change in ways words sometimes cannot. Use your voice in your own way."

That night, as Maya lay in bed, her mother's words echoed in her mind. She decided to create a series of paintings that reflected the struggles of the community, using her art as a means of advocacy. With each stroke, she poured her heart into the canvas, telling stories of resilience, hope, and the fight for justice.

The Exhibition

Weeks later, Maya organized an art exhibition titled "Voices of the Voiceless," showcasing her work at a local gallery. She invited community members, activists, and even her mother's colleagues. As the opening night approached, excitement mingled with anxiety; Maya wondered if her art would resonate with others as deeply as it did with her.

The night of the exhibition, the gallery buzzed with energy. Attendees moved from piece to piece, captivated by the raw emotion and powerful narratives behind each painting. Maya stood by her mother, watching as people engaged in conversations sparked by her artwork. For the first time, she felt the power of her own voice.

When the event concluded, Elena beamed with pride. "You did it, Maya! You've started a dialogue," she said, pulling her daughter into a warm embrace. "Your art is advocating for change in a way I could never express."

A New Path

Inspired by the exhibition's success, Maya began collaborating with local advocacy groups, using her art to raise awareness about social issues. She discovered that her passion and her mother's mission could coexist, blending creativity with activism. Maya's art became a bridge between communities, fostering understanding and empathy.

As she grew into adulthood, Maya found her unique voice in the world of advocacy, using her talents to amplify the stories of those often unheard. She continued to support her mother's work, not by speaking at rallies but by painting murals in underserved neighborhoods, each one a tribute to the resilience of the human spirit.

Legacy of Change

Years later, as Maya stood before a mural depicting the struggles and triumphs of her community, she realized how far she had come. She had embraced her identity as the advocate's daughter, not by replicating her mother's path but by forging her own. Elena, now a mentor to many, remained her greatest inspiration, encouraging her to continue pushing boundaries through art.

In that moment, Maya understood that advocacy could take many forms. Whether through words, art, or community engagement, the essence of fighting for justice remained the same. She had learned to honor her mother's legacy while crafting her own story, and together, they continued to make a difference in the world.

CHAPTER SIXTY

THE JOURNEY OF BELONGING

In the heart of a bustling city, where gleaming skyscrapers towered over modest homes, lived a young girl named Amina. She belonged to a poor family, her father working long hours as a mechanic and her mother managing a small roadside stall selling vegetables. Despite their struggles, Amina's home was filled with love and laughter, a sanctuary amid the chaos of the world outside.

A Dream in the Making

Amina had a dream: to become a doctor. She had seen too many in her community suffer from ailments that could be treated with proper care, and she wanted to make a difference. Every evening, after helping her parents, she would study under the dim light of a flickering bulb, her textbooks worn but cherished. Her determination burned brighter than her circumstances.

Her parents, aware of her aspirations, worked tirelessly to support her education. They often sacrificed their own needs to ensure Amina had school supplies and the chance to attend tutoring sessions. They believed in her dream, even when the weight of their financial struggles threatened to dim her hopes.

A Chance Encounter

One fateful day, while volunteering at a local health camp, Amina met Dr. Singh, a compassionate physician who dedicated his life to serving underprivileged communities. Impressed by Amina's eagerness to learn and her insightful questions, he became a mentor to her. He encouraged her to apply for a scholarship at a prestigious medical school, believing she had the potential to excel.

Amina felt a mix of hope and fear. The scholarship represented a chance to change her life, but the thought of leaving her family and community was daunting. Yet, she knew that to reach her destination, she needed to take this leap of faith.

The Application

With Dr. Singh's guidance, Amina meticulously prepared her scholarship application. She poured her heart into the essay, detailing her experiences, struggles, and dreams. She wanted the selection committee to understand that her journey was not just about academic excellence; it was about belonging and the responsibility she felt to her community.

As the deadline approached, Amina's excitement was tinged with anxiety. She knew that many students from affluent backgrounds were also vying for the scholarship. But she held onto the belief that her story mattered.

The Waiting Game

Weeks passed after submitting her application, and Amina was consumed with uncertainty. During this time, her parents continued to support her, reminding her that regardless of the outcome, they were proud of her efforts. They emphasized the importance of resilience and the value of hard work, teaching her that belonging was about more than financial status; it was about heart and dedication.

One evening, as Amina was helping her mother at the vegetable stall, a letter arrived. Her heart raced as she tore open the envelope. The words jumped off the page: she had been awarded the scholarship! Overwhelmed with joy, she rushed to share the news with her family, their small home filled with cheers and tears of happiness.

The New Chapter

With her scholarship secured, Amina embarked on a new journey to medical school. The transition was challenging; she felt out of place among peers who had lived lives far removed from her own. However, she carried her roots with her—each lesson learned from her parents and her community fueled her ambition.

As she navigated the rigorous demands of medical school, Amina formed bonds with fellow students and mentors. She discovered that her experiences gave her a unique perspective, allowing her to connect with patients on a deeper level. Her sense of belonging evolved from one defined by financial circumstances to one rooted in shared experiences and empathy.

A Full Circle

Years later, Amina graduated at the top of her class, her heart swelling with pride as she received her diploma. She returned to her community, not just as a doctor but as a beacon of hope for those who had once felt limited by their circumstances.

Amina established a free clinic, ensuring that quality healthcare was accessible to everyone, regardless of their financial situation. She often reflected on her journey and the importance of belonging—not just to a family or a community, but to a vision of a better world.

Through her work, Amina proved that dreams could be achieved through hard work and resilience. Her story became a source of inspiration for countless others, showing that no matter where you start, with determination and a sense of belonging, you can reach your destination.

CHAPTER SIXTY-ONE

MY SWEET HOME

In the heart of the valley where the wildflowers bloom,
Stands a humble dwelling, filled with warmth and room.
The laughter of loved ones dances through the air,
Each corner tells a story, each wall a whispered prayer.
Morning light spills softly through the windowpanes,
Casting golden shadows on the weathered frames.
The aroma of spices wafts from the kitchen wide,
Where meals are shared together, with love as our
guide.
The creak of the floorboards sings a familiar tune,
A melody of memories under the watchful moon.
In the garden, the roses blush with vibrant grace,
A tapestry of colors, a cherished, sacred space.
Through storms and through sunshine, we gather and
grow,
In the sanctuary of comfort, where true affection flows.
Though the world may be vast, and the road may be
long,
In my sweet home, I find where my heart belongs.
When shadows gather round, and the night draws
near,
I feel the gentle heartbeat of those I hold dear.
In every whispered secret, in every shared sigh,

My sweet home is a treasure, where love will never die.

CHAPTER SIXTY-TWO

RADIENCE OF DURGA

MAHISHASURAMARDINI

In the heart of the cosmos, where shadows retreat,
A lioness roars, her power replete.
With ten arms outstretched, she wields fierce light,

Goddess Durga, in the battle of night.
Cloaked in the colors of dawn's gentle grace,
She dances through storms, a celestial embrace.
Her eyes, like stars, pierce the veil of despair,
A promise of strength in each whispered prayer.
From mountains she rises, the timeless protector,
Each heartbeat a rhythm, each breath a connector.
With a crown of the moon and a heart of pure fire,
She fuels the spirit, ignites our desire.
In the face of the tempest, she stands ever bold,
A tale of resilience in legends of old.
With love as her armor, she shatters the chains,
In her fierce embrace, our courage remains.
O Durga, divine in your boundless grace,
Guide us through darkness, in our sacred space.
With your blessings, we rise, unbroken, unbowed,
In the strength of your spirit, we stand proud and loud.

CHAPTER SIXTY-THREE

THE LAST DAY OF HIGHER SECONDARY SCHOOL

The final bell rang, echoing through the corridors of Maplewood High, marking the end of an era. For Maya, it felt surreal. She stood by her locker, staring at the fading photographs pinned to the inside—snaps from school events, candid moments with friends, and little notes of encouragement exchanged over the years.

As students poured out into the bright afternoon sun, laughter and shouts filled the air. Maya's heart raced with a mix of excitement and nostalgia. This was it—the last day of high school.

Her friends, Raj and Anya, found her amidst the crowd. Raj was holding a stack of yearbooks, his grin wide. "Who's ready to make some memories?" he teased, winking.

"We're not done yet," Anya added, her arms full of snacks for their planned picnic. "We still have the whole day ahead of us!"

They decided to head to their favorite spot—a small hill behind the school where they often escaped for quiet moments or to study under the sprawling oak tree. The climb was steep, but they didn't mind; each step felt symbolic, a farewell to the familiar path they had walked for years.

Once at the top, they spread out their picnic blanket and sat in a comfortable silence for a moment, soaking in the view of the school below. "Can you believe we're actually done?" Maya asked, her voice barely above a whisper.

"It's a little scary," Raj admitted. "But it's also kind of amazing."

Anya pulled out a yearbook and flipped to the first page. "Let's write messages for each other! Future memories to look back on."

They took turns writing heartfelt notes, reminiscing about inside jokes and shared dreams. As Maya wrote, she reflected on how much she had grown. High school had been a whirlwind of late-night cramming, awkward dances, and cherished friendships. The thought of leaving it all behind felt heavy.

After they finished, Maya glanced at the time. "We should probably head back for the farewell assembly."

As they made their way down the hill, they stumbled upon a group of classmates taking photos. "Join us!" one of them called out, and soon they were all posing, arms slung around each other, smiles wide. It was a moment frozen in time.

The assembly hall buzzed with energy. Teachers shared heartfelt speeches, and students recounted their favorite memories. When it was Maya's turn to speak, she felt a wave of nerves. Standing at the podium, she looked out at her classmates—some she had known since kindergarten, others who had become like family.

"I can't believe this day has come," she began, her voice shaking slightly. "High school has been a rollercoaster ride. We've laughed, cried, and grown together. And while we're all heading our separate ways, I know the memories we've made will stay with us forever."

The applause that followed filled her with warmth. As the assembly ended, Maya and her friends stepped outside, where a sea of balloons and banners awaited them.

"Now for the best part," Raj announced, pulling out a confetti cannon. "Let's celebrate!"

With a loud pop, confetti filled the air, shimmering in the sunlight. Students cheered, their laughter ringing out as they embraced the moment. Maya felt a sense of freedom wash over her—this was not just an end but a beginning.

As the sun began to set, casting a warm glow over the school, Maya and her friends stood together, their arms linked. "To us," Anya said, raising an imaginary toast.

"To us!" they echoed, their hearts full of hope and anticipation for the future.

As they walked away from the school, Maya glanced back one last time. The building, once a source of anxiety and stress, now felt like a cherished friend. She knew that while this chapter was closing, a new adventure awaited just around the corner.

And with that thought, she took a deep breath, ready to embrace whatever came next.

CHAPTER SIXTY-FOUR

THE LAST DAY OF LIFE

The sun rose slowly over the horizon, painting the sky in hues of orange and pink. For Thomas, it was just another day—or so he thought. As he sat on his porch with a cup of coffee, he felt a strange sense of clarity settle over him. Today was different. Today was the last day he would spend on Earth.

It had been a week since he received the diagnosis—terminal illness, a few months left at most. The news had rocked his world, but now, in the quiet of the morning, he found a sense of peace. He knew he wanted to spend his last hours doing the things that mattered most.

After finishing his coffee, Thomas decided to take a walk through the small town he had called home for decades. The streets were familiar, each corner holding a memory. He waved to Mr. Johnson, the elderly man who lived down the block, and shared a few words about the weather. It felt good to connect, even in such a small way.

His first stop was the bakery where he had gotten his morning croissant for years. The warm, buttery smell wrapped around him like a hug. He ordered his favorite pastry and, instead of rushing off, he took a moment to sit and enjoy it, savoring each bite.

As he sat there, he watched the life around him—the laughter of children playing, the chatter of friends catching up over coffee. It reminded him of the vibrant moments that made life so precious. With a smile, he made a mental note to cherish every second.

Next, he headed to the park, where he had spent countless afternoons. The sun filtered through the leaves, creating a patchwork of light on the grass. He found a bench and sat, soaking in the beauty of the day. It was here that he pulled out a small notebook and began to write letters to his family and friends.

"Dear Sarah," he began, pen trembling slightly. He poured his heart into the letter, expressing gratitude for her friendship and recounting the memories they had shared. Each word felt like a lifeline, a connection he wanted to leave behind.

As the sun climbed higher in the sky, Thomas wandered to the local library. He loved books, and he often lost himself in their pages. Today, however, he wanted to share his love of literature with others. He approached the librarian, Mrs. Reynolds, and suggested a small reading session for kids.

"Let's inspire the next generation," he said, his eyes sparkling with enthusiasm. Together, they gathered a group of children, and he read them a story about adventure and friendship. Their laughter filled the room, and for a moment, Thomas felt immortal, as if he were weaving his spirit into their joy.

The day continued, each moment a reminder of the beauty that surrounded him. As evening approached, he headed home, reflecting on everything he had done. He realized how important it was to leave a legacy—not of wealth or possessions, but of love and memories.

Back on his porch, he pulled out his phone and called his family. As they spoke, he shared stories from his life, lessons learned, and moments cherished. They laughed and cried together, the bond between them growing even stronger.

When the sun began to set, painting the sky in vibrant colors, Thomas felt a sense of fulfillment wash over him. He sat quietly, listening to the sounds of the evening—the rustle of leaves, the distant laughter of neighbors, the chirping of crickets. He felt at peace.

As darkness enveloped the sky, Thomas closed his eyes and reflected on the life he had lived. He thought of the love he had given and received, the laughter, the tears, and the beauty of every fleeting moment.

In those final moments, he whispered a simple prayer of gratitude for the life he had led. With a smile on his lips, he took a deep breath, feeling the warmth of the world around him. And then, with a gentle sigh, he let go, embracing the unknown with an open heart.

CHAPTER SIXTY-FIVE

TRUE FRIENDSHIP

In the quiet moments, where laughter gleams,
A bond is woven, stitched with dreams.
Through storms and sunshine, hand in hand,
True friendship blooms, like flowers in sand.
With whispered secrets under the stars,
We share our journeys, our hopes, our scars.
In silence we gather, no words need to flow,
For in each other's eyes, we already know.

When shadows gather and doubts take flight,
You're the beacon, my guiding light.
In every struggle, you stand by my side,
A steadfast anchor, a faithful guide.
We dance through the seasons, both joyful and sad,
In moments of triumph, in times that are bad.
With laughter that echoes, and tears that we share,
True friendship's a treasure, beyond compare.
So here's to the ones who know us so well,
Who lift us up high when we stumble and fell.
In the tapestry of life, stitched with care,
True friendship endures, a bond rare and fair.

About The Author

I'm Subhasmita Panda a second year student of Bachelor of Technology . I was born in the year 2005.After I was born from my mother's womb and brought up by my mother, when I slowly started to know the world, then my thoughts and dreams of becoming a poet were guarding in my mind. With the blessings of God and the help of my father, I continued to move forward and My father and mother continued to help and cooperate with me. After that, at the age of 18, I discovered a book and wanted to become a role model for people, and my dream came true. As well as being a poet, I am also a good painter who has gained recognition by participating in competitions across the country and abroad and got certificate and madals from National and International level also.

With a background in engineering, I approaches my writing with a unique perspective, merging creativity with analytical thinking. This blend allows me to craft compelling stories that resonate deeply with readers, encouraging them to reflect on my own experiences and emotions.

When I'm not writing or immersed in my studies, I enjoys painting, exploring nature, and engaging in literary discussions with fellow aspiring authors. I believes in the importance of community and collaboration in the creative process. I looks forward to continuing my journey as a writer, sharing my stories, and inspiring others to find my voices. I hopes that my work not only entertains but also sparks conversations that lead to understanding and empathy.

At last I have so much inspiration for the next generation, and if they continue to make their own wishes and dreams such a myth, they may all be left behind but the mother who gave birth to them and the father who brought them up can never go away.

Do Hard Work And Get Success

Success is not merely a destination; it is the culmination of dedication, perseverance, and relentless hard work. This journey is often filled with challenges and setbacks, yet each obstacle presents an opportunity for growth and learning. Through disciplined effort and a steadfast commitment to one's goals, individuals can transform their aspirations into reality.

In this book, I explore the profound connection between hard work and success, illustrating that true achievement is built on the foundation of determination and resilience. From personal anecdotes to inspiring stories, I delve into the principles that drive success, emphasizing that the path may be arduous, but the rewards are undeniably worthwhile.

Ultimately, this journey serves as a reminder that success is not just about reaching the finish line—it's about the lessons learned along the way and the strength gained through perseverance. By embracing hard work and remaining steadfast in our pursuits, I can unlock my true potential and create a lasting impact on the world around me.

The Essence Of Happiness

Happiness is a multifaceted concept, shaped by our experiences, relationships, and inner perceptions. At its core, it emerges from a deep sense of connection—both with ourselves and the world around us. Joy often resides in the simple moments: the laughter shared with loved ones, the tranquility found in nature, and the satisfaction of pursuing passions. Cultivating gratitude and mindfulness enhances our appreciation for these moments, allowing us to savor the present. Furthermore, the act of giving and supporting others fosters a profound sense of fulfillment. Ultimately, happiness is not a destination but a continuous journey of self-discovery, resilience, and meaningful engagement with life. By embracing this journey, we unlock the potential for enduring joy, woven into the fabric of our everyday existence.

The Pursuit Of Well-being

What is good for me encompasses a holistic approach to well-being, integrating physical, mental, and emotional health. It begins with nourishing my body through balanced nutrition and regular exercise, fostering energy and vitality. Equally important is nurturing my mind, engaging in lifelong learning, and practicing mindfulness to cultivate resilience and clarity. Social connections play a vital role in my well-being, as meaningful relationships provide support and joy. Engaging in activities that spark my creativity and passion enriches my life, offering a sense of purpose and fulfillment. Ultimately, what is good for me is a harmonious blend of self-care, personal growth, and connection, creating a foundation for a balanced and fulfilling life.

Thank You

Gratitude
is the
heart's
memory.

Thank you for being
part of this journey.
Wishing you love and success
in everything you do.

A small act of gratitude can make a big difference in
someone's day.